I0615143

The Sun Gawks

RAYMOND HAN

Little Rocket Books

Website: www.raymondhan.net
E-mail: han.raymond@hotmail.com

Little Rocket Books, Singapore
ISBN: 978-981-11-4412-7 (pbk.)

National Library Board, Singapore Cataloguing in Publication Data
Name(s): Han, Raymond, 1958-
Title: The Sun Gawks / Raymond Han.
Description: Singapore : Little Rocket Books, 2017. | Sequel to "Where the
Wind Blows".
Identifier(s): OCN 998851872 | ISBN 978-981-11-4412-7 (paperback)
Subject(s): LCSH: Singaporean fiction. | Dictators--Fiction. | Young adults--
Fiction.
Classification: DDC S823--dc23

DEDICATION

To Life, Liberty and the Pursuit of
Happiness.

"No notice is taken of a little evil, but when it increases it strikes the eye."

Aristotle

ALSO BY RAYMOND HAN

WHERE THE WIND BLOWS

THE GOLDELL PRISM

SPICE OF LIFE:
SINGAPORE SHORT STORIES

ESSENTIAL GUIDE TO O-LEVEL ENGLISH
COMPOSITION

"To every thing there is a season,
and a time to every purpose under the
heaven:
A time to be born, and a time to die."

Ecclesiastes 3:2

ACKNOWLEDGMENTS

Thanks again to my wife, Cindy, for being my
pillar of support in this my third novel.

VISIT THE AUTHOR'S WEBSITE

Find out more about Raymond Han on his
Website
at www.raymondhan.net

CHAPTER 1

Kuan Hee paced the corridor outside the delivery ward on level two of Kandang Kerbau Hospital. He was in a pensive mood and thoughts were running wild in his mind. He had elected not to witness the birth of his first child with Lina—he was afraid of blood, and seeing blood would send him into a squeamish state—so he could not fault others. How he regretted this decision. If only he had mustered the courage to face up to his Achilles' heel.

But, it was too late. Lina had been in the delivery suite for ages. No one had come out since. Kuan Hee was getting frantic, but he suppressed the urge to barge into the room.

Then the door swung open and a gaggle of nurses and attendants waded out.

Kuan Hee wanted to push past them, but stopped. Someone had come out, cradling a baby in her arms—his daughter!

"Mr Wang, congratulations," said a nurse. "The baby is beautiful."

"She sure is," Kuan Hee exclaimed. "She sure is. Can I hold her?"

"Not yet, Mr Wang," said the nurse. "She needs to go

to the observation ward first. You can take a look from the corridor window later." Having said her piece, the nurse strode off, not giving Kuan Hee a chance to reply.

Next to come out of the delivery suite was Lina, looking pale on a gurney. He grabbed her nearest hand and squeezed it. He searched for words in his mind, but none came. She understood his thoughts and flashed a weak smile.

In Ward thirty-two on level three, the pair found themselves alone in the four-bedded room.

"Sorry, dear. Sorry."

"It's alright. I'm fine. Really. Did you see the baby?"

"Yes, beautiful—very beautiful."

"Yeah, I thought so too. Looks exactly like you."

"No, *lah*. More like you. She's got your big eyes and small nose."

"Too bad, Mum and Dad aren't here. They'd be thrilled to bits."

"Kuan Hee. It's been ages since we last spoke to them. Why haven't they contacted us?"

"You know my Dad's doing top-secret work for the US government. He would disappear for months at a stretch. Sometimes Mum would get all upset with him. But, they are together now. She would take good care of him. They should be OK, I guess."

"I'd love for them to see our baby."

"Soon, dear. Soon."

"So are we set on Huei Huei for her name? Or should we continue waiting for your father and mother?"

"Let's wait a little longer, dear. I'll try to contact them again."

The door to the ward flew open and two uniformed women stood in the doorway. One had a clipboard in her hand and the other was holding the handles of a wheelchair.

"Lina Goh. Ms Lina Goh, is it?" asked one.

"Yes," said Lina.

"You have to come with us, Ms Goh," said the woman.

"Why, where to?" asked Kuan Hee.

"Are you the husband?" said the woman.

"Yes, she's my wife," said Kuan Hee.

The woman tore off a sheet of paper from the clipboard and thrust it into Kuan Hee's hand.

"Here. Take this. Your wife needs to follow us. We are taking her to the Transition Centre in Tampines."

In Kuan Hee's hand was a Ministry of Social Affairs notice ordering Lina to report to the Transition Centre for follow-up. These two women were working for the Ministry. The Transition Centre was a euphemism for detention centre. They were going to take her there for compulsory tubal ligation.

"But, my wife is a university undergraduate," said Kuan Hee.

"Not here—in this form. It says 'Highest Standard Passed: Polytechnic'," said the woman.

"She's merely on a hiatus. She's going to rejoin the university after the delivery," said Kuan Hee.

"That's not for me to decide. You can file an appeal," said the woman. Much to Lina's chagrin, the woman grabbed her and sat her in the wheelchair.

"Sorry, but we have to hurry along," said the woman. Ignoring the pair's protests, they marched Lina off in the corridor towards the lift.

"Kuan Hee, my smartphone—my smartphone," said Lina.

"You don't need that where you are going," snapped the woman.

"I'll lodge a complaint," shouted Kuan Hee.

"Go ahead. Be my guest," said the woman. "Everyone says the same thing to me. But nothing happens to me. By the way, my name's Sanita."

These Singaporeans, she muttered under her breath. *They never tire of complaining.*

Kuan Hee stood helpless, clenching the slip of paper.

Having collected his thoughts, he whipped out his iPhone and googled the address given on the paper. The Centre stood between Tampines Industrial Street sixty-one and Tampines Place. *It's behind the row of temples in Old Tampines Road,* thought Kuan Hee. *Why, that's the old foreign workers' dormitory. They must have converted it into a holding centre for non-graduates.*

Kuan Hee and Lina had passed the building many times on their way to the Tampines hub of shopping centres where they would spend many a weekend browsing the shops and taking their lunch.

This is a piece of shit, Kuan Hee thought. *Holding people against their will and forcing them to undergo sterilisation. What government would do such a thing! This is not the twentieth century, for God's sake.*

But this was the reality in Singapore. In 2035, a new government under the Green Party had been elected into power, sweeping all but eight constituencies. The party could enact any law it deemed fit, for it had a two-third majority in Parliament. And enact a slate of new laws it did. The Green Party government thought well of graduates and feted them with benefits and status. It scorned non-graduate mothers. These mothers were separated from their spouses and their babies, and housed in a detention centre to await compulsory sterilization. The freedom of the individual was sacrificed in favour of the collective wellbeing of the state.

At the helm of the Green Party was Ong Chwee Seng, a political veteran who had been detained along with other political leaders under the Tee regime in 2030. The Tee regime's departure had been greeted with glee. Nobody expected the regime's excesses to be reprised in the new Green Party government—until it was too late. The Green Party government had four more years to do more damage to the country. And nobody could do a thing about it. After all, the party was elected in a democratic process. The people reaped what they sowed.

Kuan Hee slid into his father's Honda Accord, chose a cruising speed and put the car into autopilot. He needed to think, and weaving in and out of traffic would distract his thoughts. The car moved out of the hospital grounds and entered the main road.

The last five years had seen a quantum leap in the adoption of technology. After a lengthy fifteen-year trial run, buses and cars were finally allowed to ply the roads on autopilot. Heavy vehicles had to endure a longer wait. But autopilot wasn't for anyone in a hurry. At cruising speeds of less than fifty kilometres an hour, journeys on it were a tad slow for impatient Singaporeans. However, it fitted Kuan Hee's present need. He had to figure out a way to get Lina released from the detention centre—and quickly. She would be scared stiff in such a cold unfriendly environment. And to make things worse, she had just delivered! She was in no state to endure shock.

Oh yes, the Ministry of Social Affairs, thought Kuan Hee. *That's where I should be going now.*

He tapped the autopilot screen on the dashboard and selected the ministry on the map. Then he leaned back in the driver's seat.

The visit to the Ministry of Social Affairs was a futile exercise. He received the merry-go-round treatment. The staff pointed him to the Ministry of Family and Children, which in turn redirected him to the Prime Minister's Office. He learnt the Prime Minister's Office had issued the directive to the Ministry.

Gosh! I've forgotten to see Huei Huei, thought Kuan Hee. *But it's too late to go back. Visiting hours would be in the evening.*

The iPhone beeped. A notification had just come in from the Ministry of Defence's app. It was a mobilization exercise. Kuan Hee had to report to camp immediately.

"Drat!" said Kuan Hee under his breath. "What a day!"

Kuan Hee stared in disbelief at the iPhone screen.

Should I or shouldn't I? he thought. He was in two minds. He could make a quick detour to the reporting centre—an army camp in Portsdown Road—and then get out of the place in no time. He needn't bring along his army wear for they were stored in his camp, ready for him whenever he reported to camp. It was a paid service he had subscribed to, for the sake of convenience.

It's settled then, Kuan Hee told himself. He switched off the car's autopilot and drove at top speed to Portsdown Road.

CHAPTER 2

Portsdown Road meandered on an undulating terrain. Sitting atop was a row of two-storey buildings, which had seen active service during the colonial years. The roofs of the buildings stuck out like the jagged edge of a serrated knife against the clear blue sky, ready to slice into the hearts and minds of its unsuspecting visitors today.

There was a long line of cars waiting to get through the main gate. Reservists on foot streamed past the cars. *There must be at least a brigade of men gathering here today,* thought Kuan Hee. He had not seen such a large congregation of soldiers since Exercise Surprise two years ago. He parked the Honda some distance from the main building and took in the view.

At one end of the parade square were rows of three-tonners. The louvred doors of the building in front of the square were folded back, revealing counters and shelves of army gear. It seemed to be a warehouse. Instead of soldiers, there were khaki-uniformed men manning these counters. From their accent, Kuan Hee could tell they were foreigners. The Green Party government had begun hiring foreigners for non-essential services in the army. With a local resident population of five million and a nonresident strength of three million, this new government policy seemed plausible. There were more khaki-uniformed men sitting at a line of GS tables perpendicular to the building. They were registering the attendance of reservists who had arrived earlier.

Kuan Hee kept an eye out for familiar faces but saw none. *This doesn't seem like a mobilization exercise for my battalion,* Kuan Hee thought. Then he frowned. As the reservists cleared the registration process, they were ushered into the building where soldiers at check-out counters handed out back-packs, uniforms, socks, underwear, foot powder and boots to them. These were brand new issue. Not since their recruit days had these reservists seen such stuff dispensed to them in an assembly line.

It's not a routine reporting exercise this time, Kuan Hee thought. *I've made a wrong decision.* He was right. The queue of reservists snaked into the warehouse and then out the other end into—more three-tonners waiting for them behind the building. With their human cargo safely aboard, the three-tonners rumbled out of the camp through the back gate. The reservists had tried in vain to find out where they were being ferried. There had been no briefing at the camp. It was merely a check-in and check-out process.

As Kuan Hee sat on the packed three-tonner with other strangers, he tried to make sense of the route the truck was taking, oblivious to the chatterings of those around him. A three-tonner behind the truck blocked much of the view of the road. Buildings, trees and open spaces fleeted past him. As the truck rumbled through kilometre upon kilometre of road, he realized it was heading either to Khatib Camp or Nee Soon Camp.

"For sure, it's going to Nee Soon Camp," said a reservist. "Khatib Camp is too small to hold so many of us."

"How long are they going to keep us there?" grumbled

another. "I've a business to run. I'm a one-man show."

"Why no advance notice?" complained a third man.

Kuan Hee had come unprepared too. He hadn't gotten a chance to see his Huei Huei. He was supposed to try to get Lina out of the detention centre. It was a bad day set to become worse. What was the intention of the military, calling up so many reservists at one go? Was war imminent? Or was a big-scale exercise in the works? No one on the three-tonner had the answer.

Yes, Germaine. Why didn't I think of her? Kuan Hee thought. He took out his iPhone, sought out her name and tapped furiously on its screen. Germaine Goh was Lina's paternal cousin. She had spent several years in the United Kingdom, first for her degree in business administration, then for her post-graduate studies. She had recently returned to Singapore. Being three years older than Lina, she was like an elder sister, for Lina had none.

Done! Kuan Hee told himself. *Now just have to wait for news from Germaine.* He pocketed his iPhone.

Kuan Hee regretted not taking along little Busy the robot housefly. It could have given him a first-hand view of Lina. He would have been able to talk to her through little Busy. *Aiyah! It's my work,* he thought. *I've always been immersed in my work. Too engrossed to think clearly.* Kuan Hee was now a research assistant at Temasek University where he graduated last year. He was attached to the Cyborg Intelligence Unit, hoping to hone his skills at nanotechnology—his father's speciality.

The three-tonner rocked as it climbed a slope. Then it slowed down. The shops lining the side of the road came into view. Then the arched gates of Nee Soon Camp loomed overhead. The three-tonner had reached its destination.

Jumping down the three-tonner, Kuan Hee surveyed the surroundings. Nee Soon Camp was an unfamiliar place. He had spent most of his national service days in SAFTI in Jurong. Although he had occasion to visit the nearby Dieppe Barracks, it was only a brief stay for training.

"Third Sergeant Wang Kuan Hee," shouted a voice. Kuan Hee woke from his thoughts. "Third Sergeant Wang Kuan Hee," went the voice again.

Kuan Hee snapped to attention and raised his arm.

"Third storey, Block C, Room B," said the voice. It belonged to a senior NCO.

The third storey was where ghosts were reported to have caused fear to fellow soldiers over the past forty years. Kuan Hee had heard stories of ghosts appearing in the middle of the night, turning on water taps in the toilets. Online forums also told of recruits jumping off the third storey of the building. *Is this building one of those mentioned? Are these recruits still haunting the place?* Kuan Hee wondered. Goose pimples appeared on his arms, unhinging his thoughts momentarily.

Along with other reservists occupying the room on the third storey, Kuan Hee inspected the metal cupboard and the bunk. He was to sleep on the lower of two bunks. He dumped his belongings into the cupboard and, like the other occupants, returned to fiddling with his smartphone. It was the one ubiquitous preoccupation of people these days.

So far, there had been no flurry of activity consistent with the urgency of the call-up exercise. Then the order came for a briefing in the parade square at 2:00 p.m. When everyone had assembled, an officer mounted the concrete platform in front of the flagpoles. His voice boomed through the speakers in the big parade square.

"Gentlemen, you must all be wondering why you have been called up this time," said the officer. "I am here to provide the answers—clear your doubts, so to speak."

Instead of clearing the doubts of the audience, he rambled on about the virtues of performing reservist duties at a time when the country was at peace. As he droned on, he lost the attention of everyone in the square.

Then he came to the part about extending the reservists' stay in the camp. That was when the reservists were all ears.

The officer said the brigade was embarking on Exercise Panther, which would take two weeks to complete. All reservists present would be served with in-camp orders immediately. As part of a pilot programme, they would be issued with wrist tags to monitor their health in real-time.

"Must have taken the idea from Changi Prison," murmured a reservist next to Kuan Hee. "A friend of mine was wearing something like that when I visited him in prison."

"Maybe he worked in Changi Prison before he became a soldier," quipped another reservist.

"But the wrist tag is not for monitoring the health of the wearer," said the first reservist. "It is meant to track our movements. There is a GPS device embedded."

"Really?" said the second reservist.

"Seems like it," said Kuan Hee.

Kuan Hee cocked his head to get a better look at the figure on the dais. There was row upon row of reservists in front of Kuan Hee, some of whom were a head taller than him. It was difficult to see the platform clearly. But something in the figure triggered Kuan Hee's memory. He had seen this man before—somewhere. He stretched his neck. This guy had close-cropped hair and a brawny frame. And the way he ran his fingers over his ear. There was no mistaking it. It was—horror of horrors—Major David Foo in person! Kuan Hee blinked; for a moment he couldn't believe what his eyes were telling him. But, it was Major David Foo in the flesh all right. Nope. This time, Major Foo was wearing a lone star on his epaulette. The Major was now a Brigadier General! Kuan Hee stared in disbelief. *How did he become a Brigadier General?* he wondered. *This guy had been arrested after the downfall of Colonel Tee. Shouldn't he have been court-martialled?* But Kuan Hee had no ready answers to his questions. Instead of receiving punishment,

Major Foo had been promoted and now he was cockier. *Must have bootlicked his way up the ranks,* Kuan Hee consoled himself.

Two weeks—the reservists had to contend themselves with restricted movements for that long. The brigadier general told them the military had served the relevant notices on their employers. There was no need for them to contact their employers. Though it was a disruption that their employers' businesses could ill afford, in the eyes of BG David Foo, it was a necessary distraction. Moral values that the Green Party government wanted to promote were far more important than mere inconvenience to commercial enterprises. To the Green Party, it was moral values, but to those on the receiving end, it was an indoctrination programme. The Green Party, through the military, was trying to pass off the indoctrination of reservists as a routine military exercise. The reservists were not training to prepare for war. Instead, they were to learn how to become better citizens under the Green Party government.

2035 was to be a year when citizens' right to self-determination would be stomped upon. With the implementation of these wrist tags, their privacy rights were also being trampled upon. Their privacy had to be sacrificed for the good of the State. But, there wasn't any need for such a step, for terrorism fears of the 2020s had been quelled with the extermination of radical elements around the world. Since then governments had put into service specialized units, which targeted cells fomenting radical ideas. These units nipped radical cells before they had a chance to take root.

What was to lay ahead for Kuan Hee and his fellow reservists in the coming days? They did not know.

What they did know was—their smartphones were being confiscated. The camp administrators had said they were keeping the smartphones in safe custody for the reservists. But this was an outright lie. Apparently, the administrators did not want the reservists to get word out about the indoctrination programme these reservists would be undergoing. In the age of social media, was this going to be possible? Kuan Hee, like the rest of his campmates, surrendered his smartphone. He wasn't a bit worried, for he still had Lina's smartphone with him. In her hurried exit from the maternity ward, she had left behind her smartphone which was now safely in his possession. He knew he had to hide it somewhere safe from prying eyes. The camp administrators might conduct a spot check of their sleeping quarters.

Kuan Hee was not one for making conversation with others. He tended to keep to himself and spoke little, except to close friends such as Tim and Navin. But this time, he engaged in animated conversation with those who shared the room with him. He had to find out more about this call-up exercise.

Though his roommates came from different reservist units, there was one common denominator. Whether old or young, all were sniper-trained. They were from different batches ORDing in different years. That was why he did not recognize any of them. Kuan Hee learnt from one of them that the reservists occupying the adjoining rooms were signallers. *There is some semblance of order in the selection of this big heap of reservists, after all,* thought Kuan Hee. *What could be the intention of the military?* he wondered. *What is their plot?*

That night, Kuan Hee pulled the blanket over him and pretended to be asleep. He waited till his roommates were in bed. He wasn't on familiar terms with them and didn't want any of them to squeal on him. He snuck out to the corridor overlooking the parade square. He had a clear view of the surroundings, including the two staircases on both ends of the third storey. He hid in a recessed portion of the wall. Taking out Lina's smartphone, he tapped on the WhatsApp app.

WHATSAPP:
"Germaine. This is Kuan Hee. I'm using Lina's phone. Did you get to see her? How is she?" texted Kuan Hee.

There was no activity on the screen for the next few minutes. Kuan Hee was getting anxious. He could not stay out too long. There might be camp administrators making their rounds soon.

"Germaine, are you there? Please reply asap," texted Kuan Hee.
"Sorry, KH. Was in bathroom," texted Germaine. "Tried to message you pm, but there was no reply."
"My iPhone has been confiscated. I'm in reservist training now," texted Kuan Hee. "Can't talk long. How's Lina? How's the baby?"
"*IDK*," texted Germaine. "I couldn't get to see her. But the counter staff said she would undergo a surgical operation—tubal ligation—on Aug 3. We must get her out before then."
"K," texted Kuan Hee. "Little Huei Huei?"
"Huei Huei. This is the baby's name?" texted Germaine. "Don't worry. Lina's mum is taking care of her now."
"*GTG*," texted Kuan Hee.

Kuan Hee sidled into the bunk quarters. His roommates were stirring in bed; they were tired after a long day in camp.

August 3! I must get her out before August 3, thought Kuan Hee as he slid Lina's smartphone into a hidden compartment in his Crumpler backpack. Lina's smartphone was safe in it.

The next day saw khaki-uniformed men slapping wrist tags on the reservists. These were made of a flexible titanium alloy and when snapped closed, needed a detacher to open. Some electronic monitoring device had been embedded. With this wrist tag, the reservists' every move was being monitored.

Then the reservist snipers were herded up a three-tonner to the nearby Nee Soon Firing Range where they were issued with Steyr SSG 69s and live cartridges.

What would the military want with snipers this time? Kuan Hee wondered. He was to get the answer to his question today.

"For some of you, it will be the last time you get to fire a Steyr SSG 69," said a Major. He was the conducting officer for the live firing practice. The reservists who were standing in a line next to the firing points smiled. *Good, then. We can go packing up and head for home,* thought one. Then they realized another row of shooters had formed up right behind them. These men were armed with SAR25s.

"You have five seconds to run to your firing point ahead, and five seconds to shoot your target," said the Major. "Fail to do so, and you could end up dead."

He must be kidding, Kuan Hee thought. This was a reservist training practice. But the line of shooters taking aim at him and the other five snipers looked menacingly serious. At once he could hear his heart thump. *These guys mean business. I can't take chances,* thought Kuan Hee. *I've Lina to live for—and to save.*

The reservist snipers ran for their lives towards their respective firing points. A hail of gunfire echoed through the range. These were real bullets whizzing through the air behind them—not mere blanks. Kuan Hee made the spot in good time. Two others were not so lucky. When he turned, he saw them lying limp on the ground. There was blood on them. The Major's warning was for real! He wasn't mincing his words. Kuan Hee steadied his breath and fired in succession at his target, five hundred metres away. Then he put down the SSG 69. The flag above his target told him he had hit pay dirt.

Back in the bunk quarters, Kuan Hee learnt that the two fallen comrades were the ones sleeping across from him. They did not make it back alive. The room was abuzz with animated chatter. All were shaken and fearful for their lives.

"This is cold-blooded murder," said a roommate. "These guys are crazy."

"Yeah. It's madness—killing our own people instead of the enemy," said another.

"Someone should report this incident," said a third.

"We can't let them get away with murder," said the first.

"We are lucky to have made it back here alive," said Kuan Hee. "But, what about tomorrow? Will there be a repeat of today's incident?"

"*Wah piang*," said the first. "It might be my turn to die tomorrow."

"We must do something—and fast," said the second.

"We must make a getaway," said Kuan Hee. "Or we will be dead meat these few days."

"Yeah. Agree," said everyone in unison.

"Anyone familiar with this camp?" asked the first. None replied. Nee Soon Camp was home to a mishmash of military units—combat engineers, band, infantry brigade and medical corps—but not snipers.

"Too bad we don't have our smartphones with us, or we can use Google Maps' real-time terrain to guide us," said the third.

"OK. We can make do. Let's plan now," said Kuan Hee. The roommates huddled together at one of the bunks, careful not to speak above a whisper.

It was an hour after dinner that night when armed soldiers barged into the bunk quarters of Kuan Hee and his roommates. Apparently, the camp administrators had got wind of the roommates' plan to escape.

BG David Foo appeared at the doorway. He walked past the reservists and turned around. Then he scrutinized them one by one.

"Just because you are reservists—you think you can forget about discipline, is it?" said BG David Foo. "Dereliction of duty is a serious offence."

He paced the room and eyed the reservists.

"Don't know how serious it is?" said BG David Foo. "Let me show you just how serious it is." He drew his SIG Sauer P226 and shot the reservist next to him in the head. The lifeless body fell onto the floor. Kuan Hee, who was standing next to the fallen reservist, felt the blood splatter onto his temple. He stood frozen in fear. The roommate next to him wetted his pants. The liquid pooled at his feet. Another roommate cowered in a corner. These reservists had never seen death in national service. Today, they saw three in a row. It was an earth-shattering experience for them.

"Try again if you dare," said BG David Foo. "Go ahead. Make my day."

That said, BG David Foo left the room. It seemed like a page from the movies. It couldn't be real. Here was a Singaporean army officer killing one of his men at point-blank range.

Three soldiers came in with a body bag and dragged out the body. Another two soldiers stood watch outside the room. The seven remaining roommates stared at one another for a long while. They were shell-shocked.

Someone must have told on us, thought Kuan Hee. *Otherwise, the room must be bugged.*

The shooting had put paid to their plan to escape.

Nobody had the guts to bring up the proposal again—at least, not for a while. Kuan Hee decided he had to do it alone. He could not take the chance of trusting any of his roommates—not after what had happened today. By hook or by crook, he had to make his getaway—for Lina's and his sake. Time was ticking away. Today was July 24. Lina's surgical procedure would take place in ten days' time. He had no time to waste. Who could he turn to for help? Kuan Hee searched his memories for a clue. He had tried in vain to reach Tim and Navin. *Oh yes, why didn't I think of him?* Kuan Hee thought. *Brigadier General Walmsley, the American operative.*

CHAPTER 3

There was no way for Kuan Hee to contact Brigadier General Walmsley. The walkie-talkie the Brigadier had given him was lying somewhere in 79 Jalan Naung. It was impossible for Kuan Hee to lay his hands on it, for there were twelve days left in his in-camp stint. Alas, it was back to the drawing block for Kuan Hee.

There were ten of them sharing the bunk quarters when Kuan Hee arrived at Nee Soon Camp. Now there were seven. These seven snipers were confined to quarters. They were expecting punishment, for AWOL or attempting to AWOL was a serious offence in the army. Three days had passed but nothing had happened to them. It was strange the camp administrators did not send them to the Court-martial Centre in Kranji Camp.

The next morning, after breakfast, the snipers were escorted to an office three blocks away. *They are finally taking action,* Kuan Hee thought. But there wasn't the usual *hentak-kaki* march that they had expected to do before disciplinary proceedings. Instead, they were being ushered into a conference room. Standing in front of a large screen was BG David Foo.

The Brigadier General greeted the snipers warmly this

time. He gestured for all to be seated.

"I'm sending you on a secret mission," said the BG. "Do it well, and you will be rewarded. I'll also forget about the AWOL matter."

"But, bungle it, and you will face dire consequences," he continued.

The BG raised his arm and his staff placed a manila envelope and a watch in front of each sniper.

"Your individual target and destination are detailed in the sealed envelope before you," BG Foo said. "It's marked 'top secret'. Do not open the envelope now. Do it when you are alone. Remember—do not discuss your target or destination with anyone. Do you understand?"

"Yes, sir," the snipers chorused in unison.

"ETA for your destination is 19:00 today," BG Foo said. "Synchronise your watches now." With that done, he dismissed the snipers.

One by one, the snipers were led into different holding rooms, with a guard stationed outside each room.

Kuan Hee surveyed his new surroundings. The room, slightly bigger than a pantry, was furnished with a chair and a small desk placed beside a lourved window. A fan whirling on the wall provided ventilation in the room. He tried to open the window. It seemed to be nailed shut from the outside. He peered through the louvres. He saw grassy sloping ground. There was the stench of urine and faeces in the air. *I must be near a toilet or sewage system,* Kuan Hee thought. The door opened, and a soldier placed a Steyr SSG 69 and a cleaning kit on the desk. Then without a word, he left.

Kuan Hee ran his fingers along the cold barrel of the rifle and let his fingers slide on the smooth fiberglass stock. *This is new issue,* he told himself. It was rare to see new Steyr SSG 69s. The sniper rifle had gone out of production in the 2010s. There was only a limited stock of about 3,000 new units left at the time. But the SSG 69 was a fine dependable weapon. It was loads better than the ones in use in armies around the world. *How did the army get their hands on new stuff?* Kuan Hee wondered. *Did they manage to find a new factory?* Then he remembered the envelope in his hand. He tore open the flap and emptied the contents on the desk. There was a large photograph of—the President. *The BG wants me to kill the President,* Kuan Hee told himself. *Why, that low-down son of a bi*— He managed to stop himself from uttering the cuss word. Even in his thoughts Kuan Hee would not swear. *This is treason. I can't do it. I just can't do it—not in a million years,* he told himself. Yet, Kuan Hee knew he had to, for his life depended on it, unless, of course, he aborted the task right at the last moment. He had to keep his plan close to his heart, for if anyone found out, he would be killed immediately.

Next to the photograph was a map. Kuan Hee pored over it. A triangle marked the firing point he was to station himself at. It was a staircase in an HDB block in King George's Avenue. It was about five hundred metres from his target's position—the porch of the Ministry of Family and Children's main building in Tyrwhitt Road. An 'X' marked the spot his target—the President—would be standing.

Kuan Hee stood in deep thought for many minutes, oblivious to the droning of the fan. Then he opened his eyes. He knew what he had to do now. He plotted his moves for that evening in his mind. That done, he went back to reminiscing the times he spent with Lina. It was the only way he knew to remain sane in difficult times.

A guard came into the room with his Crumpler backpack. It contained his civilian clothes. He said Kuan Hee was to change into civilian attire and keep the disassembled rifle in the backpack. A magazine with five cartridges would be given to him when he left for his destination.

When the guard had left, Kuan Hee reached inside the secret compartment of the backpack. He fingered the edges of the iPhone. *Good,* he told himself. *They haven't found it.*

He resisted the urge to take it out. *There might be a hidden camera somewhere in this room,* he told himself. *Can't take the risk—not now, not yet.*

The ambient heat from the windows seemed to be subsiding. Kuan Hee glanced at his watch. It showed 5:25 p.m. Shortly he would be on his way to King George's Avenue. A guard came in with a bottle of mineral water and his dinner—a box of steamed rice with some slivers of pork and julienned cabbage. He picked at the food and took swigs of the bottled water.

Then two men entered the room. They were in civilian clothes. They took him to a van whose driver was waiting in the compound. There were several of these vehicles, and as he passed them, he inhaled the fumes from the humming engines. *These other vans must be waiting for my roommates,* Kuan Hee told himself.

The van unloaded him along King George's Avenue. The magazine was now in his trouser pocket. He looked up at the HDB block façade and then at the Ministry of Family and Children's main building in the distance. Slinging his backpack, he walked past the shops on the ground floor, keeping an eye out for overhead cameras. Then he turned the corner of the block. A staircase stood in front of him. There was a police camera perching on a pillar opposite the staircase. He walked to the back of the building. *Yes, the staircase landing is only two metres high,* Kuan Hee told himself. Seeing nobody was around, he grabbed the water pipe next to the staircase and lifted himself up to the landing. *I'll use this way to get out of the building,* he told himself. He climbed the stairs up to the seventh storey and surveyed the view. *Still too low,* he thought. He walked up to the eighth storey. Here he had a clear line of sight to the target building's porch. A wooden platform had been erected in the driveway and there were people scurrying around like ants in the distance.

Kuan Hee was sure the BG's men were keeping watch

on him from somewhere in the buildings around him. He had to act the part, pretending to be studious in his task. *They will be reporting my every move to BG Foo,* he thought. Then he smiled. *I sure can act,* he told himself. He sat down behind the parapet, out of view of everyone. His watch told him it was now 6:35 p.m. He had twenty-five minutes of idle time before his target appeared. He retrieved his iPhone from the backpack and powered on the device. *Good, there's still eighty percent battery left,* he told himself.

Kuan Hee browsed channelsingapore.com but found no reports of the deaths of NSmen. *It's as if nothing happened,* he told himself. *What a cover-up.* But online posts on social media alluding to these deaths had gone viral. The forums were alive with discussions on the matter. Everyone who commented was aghast at the horrific tactics of the military. There were pictures of the dead snipers—alone, with loved ones, and beside daughters and sons. Kuan Hee fingered the screen. These men were living and breathing just days ago. *How can a government be so cruel and bloodthirsty?* he wondered. *I should alert everyone.* He hesitated. *This is Lina's smartphone. What if she gets into trouble?* he asked himself.

Hey, facebook is foreign media, he convinced himself. *The G can't access its servers.* Then he joined in the online tirade, adding little mussels of information about the army's excesses.

"Drat this wrist tag!" Kuan Hee fumed as the wrist tag brushed against his iPhone. He had forgotten about it. It could track his every move. With it on him, he was in perpetual danger. *I will need a diamond cutter or some similar tool to cut it open,* he told himself. *Ah! Lina's elder brother should have such a tool.* Her brother worked in a company specializing in heavy machinery.

Kuan Hee stood up and peered over the parapet. The Ministry of Family and Children's grounds were crowded with people. Many were milling in the driveway. Then they were waving little flags. A limousine, and behind it, a

Volvo, entered the driveway, with two outriders in front of them. *The President is here*, Kuan Hee told himself. He snapped the magazine into place on the SSG 69. Then he steadied the rifle, taking aim at the figure in a navy blue suit. It was evening, but the ambient light was good enough for him to see his target in the crosshairs of the rifle. He took a deep breath and squeezed the trigger. A shot rang out. Then there was pandemonium in the Ministry's grounds. There were screams and shouts as people pushed and shoved to get out of harm's way. Bodyguards threw themselves around the fallen President. They bundled him into the limousine. It sped off with the Volvo trailing, and siren wailing.

Kuan Hee disassembled the rife and placed it in his Crumpler backpack. Then he recoiled in pain. He had been shot. He was bleeding in his left chest. He grabbed a packet of tissue from his backpocket and pressed it on the open wound. He grimaced and disappeared behind the parapet. Someone had taken a shot at him from a nearby building. The size of the open wound told him it was a sniper's 51mm that had lodged in his chest. *One of my roommates must have done it*, Kuan Hee surmised. *The guy's mission is to kill me off after my job is done. Thank God, he spared my life. He's a good chap, after all.*

Kuan Hee slung his backpack over his right arm and staggered down the stairs to the second storey landing. He climbed the railing and jumped onto the floor below. He could not stop, for he knew the G operatives would be coming after him any moment.

The two men who came with him in the van were a streetlamp behind him. They had seen him. He dashed across Horne Road and entered Penhas Road. He strode through the dimly lit five-foot-way of the shophouses and weaved through a line of black hearses parked behind a large building. Lavender Street was home to a cluster of funeral parlours. At the back of these buildings was a coterie of busy men and women in black. He hid behind them. His pursuers hurried past the group, eyeing every moving thing fleetingly. Then they moved into the next street.

Kuan Hee turned into Lavender Road. At the junction, a van stopped abruptly. It jolted him. Then he saw Lina's elder brother at the wheel. Kuan Hee pulled aside a sliding door and threw himself onto the floor of the van. He landed on top of his backpack and he grimaced in pain—his chest hurt. The van disappeared into the busy evening traffic, leaving Kuan Hee's pursuers perplexed.

It was the second time Lina's elder brother had come to his rescue. Earlier, on the eighth storey staircase landing Kuan Hee had texted her brother for help. He had asked him to pick him up along Lavender Street. But there was no reply from her brother. Lina had always boasted to him about how her brother had never let her down. He was just like how she had described him. Kuan Hee couldn't see where the van was heading. He didn't want to risk being seen so he kept out of sight on the floor of the van. The van cruised for many minutes. Finally, it came to a stop and the side door opened.

Lina's brother climbed into the back of the van and examined Kuan Hee's wound.

"It looks bad," he said. "It needs immediate attention, otherwise—"

"The wrist tag—it must come off. They can track us using it," said Kuan Hee.

"Not to worry," said Lina's brother. He rummaged through a large toolbox in the back of the van and retrieved a pair of cutters with long handles.

"This thing can cut through steel and titanium," he said. With a quick snap, the wrist tag broke into two pieces.

"We must hurry along," said Lina's brother. He grabbed the broken pieces and exited the back of the van. He took the wheel of the vehicle and drove furiously.

Along the way, he flung the broken pieces into a bush. "There—they can't find us now," he shouted into the back of the van.

Minutes later, the van pulled into an HDB car park.

"Come, Dr Koh is waiting for us," said Lina's brother. "Leave the backpack in the van." He helped Kuan Hee to the back of Dr Koh's clinic. It was situated in an HDB block in Hougang Avenue five. Only the doctor was in the clinic as it had closed. Lina's brother lifted Kuan Hee onto the exam table in the consultation room. Then he excused himself from the room.

"Kuan Hee, what have you gotten yourself into this time?" said Dr Koh.

"Sorry, Doctor. Have to trouble you again," said Kuan Hee.

The doctor got to work cleaning the wound and then injecting Kuan Hee with an anaesthetic.

"My, my. This is a fine piece of work. Clean shot— landed near the manubrium," said Dr Koh. "51mm— rarely seen. Must be a sniper's bullet."

Kuan Hee tried to hold back his tears as the doctor dug the forceps into his chest. The doctor twisted the instrument a few times. With the other hand, he dabbed clean gauze pads generously on the blood oozing out. Then he pulled out the forceps. He was now holding a bullet with the forceps.

"You are either very lucky, or this chap intentionally missed your vital organs," said the doctor.

Turning to Kuan Hee, Dr Koh said, "It will heal in two weeks. Lie low and don't do anything but rest."

Lina's brother returned with a clean set of clothes for Kuan Hee. "It's yours," he said. "You left it behind the last time you stayed over at the house." He helped Kuan Hee change and bundled the soiled clothes together with the bloodied gauze pads into a polystyrene bag.

Dr Koh rinsed the bullet and handed it to Lina's brother. "Here, get rid of it at once."

CHAPTER 4

The President was not the only one targeted. The local newspapers reported the deaths of the Chief Justice and the Police Commissioner. They had been shot as they arrived home. The newspapers blamed foreign elements seeking to undermine the country's interests. What stood out to Kuan Hee was the President's health. He pinched the smartphone screen to enlarge the page. The news article reported that the President had escaped life-threatening injuries and was now recuperating in hospital.

Kuan Hee smiled. He was glad he had not hurt any innocent party. Just like the sniper roommate who shot him, he had shot the President in the shoulder. He had done what BG David Foo wanted him to do—only he missed killing the President. *It isn't my fault that the shot wasn't deadly,* Kuan Hee told himself. *After all, I was standing five hundred metres away from my target.* So he reckoned the BG shouldn't be too angry with him. Hopefully, the BG would cut some slack for him and let him off, for he needed to save his Lina.

It had been two days since his assassination attempt on the President. Kuan Hee was now recovering from his wound. Lina's brother had put him up on the second level of an old shophouse unit squeezed between several units in Realty Park in Hougang. It was a mere six hundred metres from 79 Jalan Nuang. Kuan Hee could walk home in five minutes! The shophouse belonged to Lina's paternal uncle. The ground floor was rented out as a hairdressing salon. The upper floor was vacant. Kuan Hee was now in the room facing the front, from where he had a clear view of a large field, and, beyond it, Hougang Avenue two.

It is dangerous to keep using Lina's SIM card, Kuan Hee told himself. *I've got to get the Polaris SIM card from the cellar—yes, AleXander too, and not forgetting little Busy and Tizzy.*

The Polaris SIM card was named after its carrier Polaris, an orbiting satellite. It belonged to his father, Professor Wang. He had used it previously when he had a run in with the now-deceased dictator Colonel Tee.

There was the sound of footsteps outside the room. Someone was coming up the stairs. Kuan Hee kept still. He heard three taps on the door. It was Xaden—Lina's brother's teenage son. He was here to deliver his lunch.

"I need to go over to my house to get a few things," said Kuan Hee. "I can't do it alone. Can you come with me?"

"Sure. When?" Xaden asked.

"Tonight, after dinner," said Kuan Hee.

"Do I bring along anything?" said Xaden.

"Just yourself," said Kuan Hee.

Xaden left after Kuan Hee had finished eating. He had to return the tiffin carrier to his grandmother—Lina's mother. Lina's mother was the one who took care of Kuan Hee's meals. She also cooked for the extended Goh family, which included all her children and grandchildren. They would come to the flat every evening for dinner, though they lived in different places in Hougang and Sengkang HDB estates.

It was 7:15 p.m. when Kuan Hee and Xaden made their

way across the road to Jalan Naung. Kuan Hee had expected his house to be under surveillance by the G operatives so they took a longer route, moving through the terrace houses behind Jalan Naung and then entering the narrow walkway between the backs of Kuan Hee's semi-detached house and the terrace houses. The smell of *sambal belacan* permeated the air. Some household was having *belacan* for dinner. He whiffed the fragrant air and recalled his favourite *Kangkong Belacan* dish, which his mum used to prepare for him. *Gosh, I miss her cooking,* he told himself.

Kuan Hee's shoulder still hurt and Xaden had to help him up the wall. Then they jumped into the rear of 79 Jalan Nuang. The inside of the house was dark, but outside, spotlights, turned on by an automatic timer, illuminated the garden. Kuan Hee took a key from underneath a potted plant and opened the back door. The duo felt their way through the kitchen into the storeroom where Kuan Hee retrieved a ladder and carried it into the study. There, he placed it next to the floor-to-ceiling bookshelf and climbed it. He pushed twice on the end panel. It moved sideways, revealing a knob. Then, he turned the knob and the bookshelf glided to one side, revealing a hidden doorway wide enough for two men to enter.

Kuan Hee switched on the lights and motioned for Xaden to follow him down the steps. The cellar was small but there was enough space to hold three cabinets, two chairs and a table. The musty air gradually made way for cooled air as a concealed air-conditioning unit kicked in. Kuan Hee opened a cabinet and AleXander, the two robots shone in the illumination. It was as if they were delighted to see him again. He placed them on the table. Next, he retrieved little Busy the housefly and Tizzy the dragonfly. He placed their remote controls on the table. He bent down and took a metal box from the bottom shelf.

"What's in the box?" asked Xaden. Kuan Hee opened

the box. There were six little rockets lined up neatly in it.

"These look like toy rockets," said Xaden. "They must be fun to play with."

"They may be small, but they are deadly—definitely not playthings," said Kuan Hee. "Each rocket can blow a hole in an army tank."

"Wow! Really? And these are neat stuff," said Xaden, fingering the two robots. "How do we switch them on? Are these the remote controls for them?"

"Meet Alex and Xander the intelligent robots," said Kuan Hee. "Together, they are called AleXander. There aren't any switches. They respond to oral instructions."

"But, they are not moving or responding to us," said Xaden.

"That's because they run on solar power," said Kuan Hee. "And they have been holed up in this cellar for a few months, so their energy level is near zero. That's why they are still."

"Is that so?" said Xaden. He was clearly mesmerized. He had never laid eyes on such handsome robots. They were different from the ones he had seen in shops and on television. "What are these?" said Xaden, pointing to the metal insects.

"This is little Busy the housefly, and that is Tizzy the dragonfly," said Kuan Hee. "They are intelligent drones, capable of eavesdropping on conversations."

"You mean they have microphones on them? But they are so small!" said Xaden.

"It's the wonder of technology—state of the art stuff—my Dad's invention," said Kuan Hee. "They also have night vision capability."

"Can I try them out?" asked Xaden.

"You'll get plenty of chances to play with them," said Kuan Hee. "But, not now. We have to hurry." He took the Crumpler backpack from Xaden and placed AleXander, the two flies and the remotes in it. Then he looked around for the Polaris SIM card. He remembered leaving it on the table, but it was nowhere to be seen.

"Is this what you are looking for?" asked Xaden, holding a SIM card in his hand. "I found this on the floor."

"Thanks, Xaden," said Kuan Hee. He took out Lina's smartphone and replaced the SIM card with the Polaris SIM card. He handed the backpack to Xaden. They were about to leave the cellar when Kuan Hee stopped.

"I plain forgot about BG Walmsley's walkie-talkie," Kuan Hee muttered. "Now, where did I leave it? It's not here."

"Let's go up to my bedroom," said Kuan Hee. "I need to get something."

In his bedroom, Kuan Hee opened a drawer and took out a thick wad of hundred-dollar bills. *These will come in handy,* Kuan Hee thought. He passed these to Xaden who placed them in the backpack. The ambient illumination filtering through the curtains across the balcony let him see his way around the room. He searched his cupboard, then his other Crumpler bags. The walkie-talkie was in one of the bags. He grabbed the walkie-talkie. Then he moved to the balcony and peeped through the curtains. The road in front of the gate was deserted. But he didn't want to take a chance. He gestured for Xaden to follow him out through the kitchen.

Instead of heading back to Realty Park, the duo walked past some HDB blocks and crossed Hougang Central. Then they doubled back to Hougang Avenue five where Lina lived. They had to use this circuitous route—just in case there were G operatives loitering in the vicinity looking for Kuan Hee.

There was a twelve-year difference in the duo's ages, but they seemed to get along well.

"Do you want me to take over carrying the backpack?" asked Kuan Hee.

"It isn't heavy," said Xaden. "I can manage."

As they approached the junction, Kuan Hee lowered

his head. There were cameras perched on top of metal posts next to the junction and he didn't want these to recognize him. At Lina's block, instead of using the lift, they climbed sixteen flights of stairs to Lina's flat. It was a four-roomed HDB flat, two doors away from the staircase.

"Auntie," greeted Kuan Hee. Though he and Lina had registered their marriage, they had yet to go through the customary wedding ceremony, so he would address Lina's mum this way.

"*Ah Ma,*" greeted Xaden. He lived with his parents in a four-roomed HDB flat in Sengkang but his family would gather at *Ah Ma's* house for dinner every evening.

Lina's mother led Kuan Hee to the master bedroom. This was Lina's room. She was the apple of her mother's eye and it was natural she would have the best that the family could afford—this included the master bedroom.

There she was, lying on a cotton mat laid in the middle of the queen-sized bed. Little Huei Huei was wrapped in a plain towel. She peered at him with her little eyes. It was not clear whether she recognized him.

"She can't hold things yet. She's only a week old," said Lina's mum. "You will have to put her hand in yours."

The baby made little noises as he placed her little hand in his.

"That's all she can do at the moment," said Lina's mum. "Make grunting sounds."

Kuan Hee wanted to cuddle her in his arms, but Little Huei Huei was drifting into sleep. *Another time, perhaps* Kuan Hee consoled himself. He watched her as she slept, not letting her little hand out of his. *You are so pretty; prettier than your mother,* Kuan Hee thought. Then he reminisced the times Lina and he spent together. *She'll be alright,* Kuan Hee told himself. *I'll get her out before Friday.* Friday was the day Lina had to undergo the sterilisation procedure.

Lina's mum was worried about her daughter, but she tried to hide her feelings. Kuan Hee already had a load on his mind. She didn't want to add to his worries.

Kuan Hee took out his wallet and retrieved a few pieces of hundred-dollar notes. He placed them in Lina's mother's hand.

"It's our share of the monthly expenses," he said. "I forgot, sorry."

She pocketed the money and nodded. Her eyes were getting teary. It would be good for Kuan Hee to make his exit now. Kuan Hee stood up, took a long look at little Huei Huei and bade goodbye to Lina's mum.

"Auntie," said Kuan Hee. "I'll get Lina out before Friday. I promise."

At the shophouse in Realty Park, Xaden put down the Crumpler backpack and gestured he was leaving. It was Monday the next day and he would return with Kuan Hee's lunch after school.

"It must be inconvenient for you, coming here after school," said Kuan Hee.

"No, not at all," said Xaden. "My school is just across the road from here." He pointed in the direction of Holy Innocents' High School.

"But, you live in Sengkang," said Kuan Hee.

"We lived with *Ah Ma* before we moved to Sengkang," said Xaden. "So I'm used to this place."

CHAPTER 5

Kuan Hee powered on the walkie-talkie. The battery level indicator was at the quarter mark. He would have to buy six AA batteries soon. But he was able to make a call to Brigadier Walmsley now. He hoped the Brigadier was available. He picked up the walkie-talkie. Then he stopped. There were footsteps in the staircase. Someone was here. Kuan Hee grabbed a metal rod and stood behind the door. He readied the weapon. There were three taps on the door, then silence. It couldn't be, but it was—Xaden had returned. This time he was slinging a backpack and carrying a duffel bag in his hand.

"I told my father I would keep you company for the next few days," said Xaden, "and he agreed."

"Won't it be troublesome for you?" asked Kuan Hee.

"This place is actually nearer to school," Xaden explained. He went to work laying some blankets on the floor. It would be his bed for the next couple of days. The duffel bag would be his pillow.

Kuan Hee sat the walkie-talkie on the table and pushed the PTT button.

"Mr Walmsley, this is Kuan Hee calling. Over."

There was no response. Kuan Hee tried again. *Perhaps, the Brigadier is away from the walkie-talkie,* Kuan Hee told himself. After some minutes, the walkie-talkie crackled with activity.

"Actually, Kuan Hee, I've been trying to get you on the walkie-talkie, but you didn't respond. Over."

"Sorry. I left the walkie-talkie in the cellar. I've gotten into a bit of trouble, Brigadier Walmsley. Over."

"What have you gotten yourself into now, Kuan Hee? Over."

Kuan Hee told the Brigadier how Lina landed in a detention centre and how he came to be a wanted man.

"I'm at my wit's end, Mr Walmsley. Please tell me what to do. Over."

"That's really quite a knot you've gotten yourself into, Kuan Hee. Let me think for a moment. Over."

There was silence over the airwaves. The minutes ticked away. Then, the Brigadier broke the silence.

"So, Kuan Hee, what do you intend to do? I want to hear what you have to say first. Over."

"I have been thinking. Perhaps, I should attempt a rescue. Over."

"How? Kuan Hee. Over."

"Storm the detention centre using AleXander the robots. Over."

"That doesn't sound like a good solution, Kuan Hee. Over."

"I thought so, too. Brigadier Walmsley. Over."

"Mmm. I suggest—I suggest. I mean, let's do it this way. Get Lina to feign illness so they will take her out of the detention centre. Rescuing her will be easier—and less messy if she is out of the place. They will take her to a hospital. Follow them or find out which hospital they take their patients to. Attempt a rescue there. Over."

"The detention centre is in Tampines. The nearest hospital is Changi General Hospital. I think they will likely take her there. Over."

"Kuan Hee, you must be sure, otherwise, it will be a waste of time—and you don't have time to waste. I suggest that you position yourself at Changi General Hospital and get someone to follow her at the detention centre. If there is a change in destination, you will know straightaway. Over."

"I understand, Brigadier Walmsley. I'll do as you say. Over."

"One more thing, Kuan Hee. I have been meaning to talk to you about your parents. Over."

"Yes, Brigadier Walmsley. I'm listening. Over."

"Listen carefully to what I have to say, Kuan Hee. Over."

"Yes. Brigadier Walmsley. Over."

"Kuan Hee. I'm afraid I have bad news to tell you. Over."

"Brigadier Walmsley. Are they hurt? Over." Though he did not say it out, Kuan Hee was preparing himself to hear the worst news. He clenched his fists.

"In a nutshell, your parents are missing. They have vanished into thin air. Over."

"How—how did it happen? Over."

"The entire research team based in Western Australia has vanished. We suspect some foreign government has abducted them. Over."

"You mean the research team my Dad is in charge of? Over."

"Yes, Kuan Hee. I'm afraid so. The team is based in Airlie Beach, on the Whitsundays Coast. We found out they have been missing for more than a year. Over."

"More than a year? You mean, Mum and Dad went missing in 2034? When did you find out, Brigadier Walmsley? Over."

"Only a week ago, Kuan Hee. I'm very sorry. Indeed very sorry that this has happened. The research unit is top secret and our contact with it has been through an agent. He had been feeding us with false information for over a year. Apparently, he had been bribed. He has gone missing too. Over."

Kuan Hee didn't know what to say. He blamed himself for not checking up on his parents regularly. He had been complacent, figuring they knew how to take care of themselves. If he had tried to contact them, he would have gotten wind of the kidnapping earlier. Now, a whole year had gone past. Any clues would have gone cold a long time ago.

"Kuan Hee, are you there? Over."

"Yes. Brigadier Walmsley. I'm here. Over."

"Don't fret, Kuan Hee. The US government is resourceful. We have people all over the world. I've agents working twenty-four seven. We'll get to the bottom of this very quickly. I promise you. Over."

"Yes, I understand. Brigadier Walmsley. Over."

"In the meantime, if you need help with Lina, let me know. Over."

"I will, Brigadier Walmsley. Good night. Over."

Xaden left Kuan Hee to his thoughts. He went to bed; he had to wake up early for school the next morning.

It was 2:30 a.m. when Kuan Hee drifted into sleep. He had let his thoughts wander—from his parents to Lina and the predicaments all of them were in now.

CHAPTER 6

Kuan Hee knew he could not act alone. He needed his pals' help. But, Tim and Navin were not responding to his WhatsApp messages. Like him, they could have been called up for reservist training. Their smartphones could also have been confiscated.

Kuan Hee had four days left to carry out his plan to rescue Lina. After he and Xaden had had lunch, they set off for the bus stop along Upper Serangoon Road. They were heading to the detention centre in Tampines. Kuan Hee had brought AleXander and the two robot flies with him. Little Busy would help him get in touch with Lina.

On board bus number 72, Kuan Hee was careful to keep his head down. The baseball cap he was wearing hid his face from the cameras aboard the bus. It was a twenty-minute ride to Tampines and the only passengers on the upper deck of the bus were far from where they were seated. Kuan Hee used the time to brief Xaden on what he had to do on Wednesday afternoon. Kuan Hee had decided that Xaden would keep watch outside the detention centre while he and his pals took up position at Changi General Hospital.

Kuan Hee and Xaden alighted fifty metres away from

the main gate of the detention centre. They walked along the perimeter of the premises to seek out the best position from which they could observe the place undetected.

The duo settled on an open spot on the edge of a large field across the road from the detention centre. *Nobody will take any notice of us here,* Kuan Hee thought. *Only little Busy will have to fly a longer distance.*

Kuan Hee had come prepared with some *layangs* he had bought from a provision shop. Fortunately, he had some experience flying *layangs* so he could teach Xaden the ropes. It was better that they busied themselves with an activity so they would not attract any unnecessary attention.

Xaden took AleXander out of the backpack and stood them on the grass. The two robots were happy to soak in the sun's energy; they had spent too long a time in the cellar. Kuan Hee released little Busy into the air. He guided Xaden who was holding the remote. Little Busy zigzagged over the road and flitted up the slope towards the dormitories. *Xaden needs more practice with the remote,* Kuan Hee thought. As they did not know where Lina had been held, they could only instruct little Busy to search the dormitory rooms one by one.

"Why did you choose Wednesday instead of Thursday or Friday?"

"As a precaution. Just in case they should change their mind and hold the sterilization procedure earlier."

"Shall I get little Busy to go up one floor?"

"Yes. Look inside the rooms via the exterior windows. It is safer for little Busy; she won't be easily noticed."

The sun was high in the sky and the August heat was sweltering. There was not a single tree in the sprawling field. Xaden was beginning to feel the effects of the heat but they had yet to find Lina. Kuan Hee almost wanted to call it a day, but Xaden insisted on continuing with the search.

"You understand I won't be with you on Wednesday,

don't you?" said Kuan Hee.

"Yes," said Xaden.

"So if you have any doubts, let me know now so I can clear them for you," said Kuan Hee. "We simply can't afford to have anything go wrong on Wednesday. Lina's safety depends on us."

"I'll try my best," said Xaden.

"Look! It's Aunt Lina," said Xaden. Little Busy was hovering over a room on the third level. Kuan Hee looked at the screen and then up at the building beyond. He pointed to a part of the building.

"That's where she is held," Kuan Hee exclaimed. "Fly little Busy up there on Wednesday. Xaden looked at where he was pointing; he nodded.

Little Busy flew through the window grilles into the room. It hovered above Lina; she was sitting on the floor in a corner of the room. She took no notice of the robot housefly.

"Lina, Lina," Kuan Hee's voice amplified through little Busy's tiny speakers. She had not heard him; she was in deep thought.

"Lina, it's me."

Lina looked around the room, then at little Busy. She beamed.

"Kuan Hee, you are here at last." She got up and peered through the small opening in the metal door. *The corridor is deserted,* she told herself. Then she sat in the corner.

"Dear, Xaden is with me. We are across the road. You look pale."

"I'm alright. It's just that I'm not used to this place. It's cold and unfriendly. What took you so long? I've been waiting for ages."

Kuan Hee recounted the happenings of the past few days.

"It's not an adventure. It's danger. How horrid of the army to treat you this way. It's the second time you have been shot in the shoulder. Does it still hurt? I wish I could see you." She rattled off in succession. She desperately wanted to see her other half, but technology had yet to reach the stage where little Busy could project a live image of Kuan Hee into the air in front of her—not just yet anyway. In the meantime, she had to contend with merely hearing his voice.

"Soon, dear, soon." Kuan Hee understood her feelings.

"Xaden, say hello to your aunt."

"Hi. Aunt Lina."

"Xaden. You're helping your uncle now."

"Yes. Aunt. He's teaching me how to use the remote. I'm to watch you on Wednesday while he waits for you at Changi General Hospital."

"Changi General Hospital?"

"I meant to tell you just now. I've a plan to get you out of this place. Report sick on Wednesday morning. Pretend you have post-natal abdominal pain. They will take you to Changi General Hospital. I'll be waiting there to rescue you."

"Kuan Hee, Xaden's only fifteen years old. You've got to be careful; don't put him in danger."

"I know, dear. He'll do the safe things. I won't put him in harm's way."

"Aunt, I'll be careful."

"Huei Huei—have you seen her? How's she?"

"Huei Huei is fine. Your mum is looking after her. She sleeps most of the time. Her fingers are so little that I had to be very gentle holding them."

"I'm looking forward to seeing her soon. This has been an exasperating time for us."

"Don't worry, we'll be together shortly."

"How's my Mu—" Lina broke off abruptly. She had heard footsteps in the corridor. There was creaking of hinges as the metal doors clanked open. "Someone is coming. It's row call again. You'd better go now."

"Remember—Wednesday morning. Wait for Xaden to

come with little Busy."

"I will. I will."

"Bye, dear." Kuan Hee caressed Lina's image on the screen

Little Busy flitted out of the sparsely furnished room into the open air and back to the duo.

"You have to monitor your aunt's every step on Wednesday," said Kuan Hee. "This means you'll be here from early morning—you can't go to school that day."

"Don't worry, I'll *ponteng* school," said Xaden.

"Good. I'm sure your father won't mind," said Kuan Hee.

Despite his attempts, Kuan Hee could not reach his pals, Tim and Navin. *If they were called up for reservist duties on the same day as me, it means they will only be released on August 6,* Kuan Hee told himself. *It will be too late. Lina's sterilization procedure is on August 3.*

If I can't get hold of Tim and Navin, I'll have to go it alone, Kuan Hee told himself. He hoped it wouldn't come to that state.

What shall I do? Kuan Hee asked himself. He realised he had to cobble up a team to do the rescue. He went to work, penning a list of trusted individuals who could help: Lina's elder brother, Germaine and Ella. Ella was Germaine's sworn sister. They had been friends since childhood days. They were inseparable. He needed one more. *Yeow Xi—why didn't I think of him?* Kuan Hee asked himself. Yeow Xi was Kuan Hee's and Lina's classmate at Holy Innocents' Primary School and his schoolmate at Victoria School. In their primary school years, the two boys had spent most of their time together at a student care centre in Hougang Avenue five, where Kuan Hee's mother was working as a teacher. Yeow Xi left for Australia after his O-levels as his father had been posted there as a country manager. After his parents returned to Singapore, he stayed back for further studies. He only came back to Singapore a month ago, after graduating from Monash University with a Master's degree. Their mothers knew each other well as Yeow Xi's mother would fetch him at the student care centre after work, and the two mothers would engage in animated conversation about their sons.

I have his phone number somewhere, Kuan Hee told himself. *It's been ages. But I'm sure he will lend a hand.*

But, Yeow Xi was unreachable. It suddenly dawned on Kuan Hee that Yeow Xi too had been called up for reservist training. It appeared that this call up exercise was a major one. All his good friends had been called up. Kuan Hee had to make do with just four helpers.

That evening, Kuan gathered Lina's brother, Xaden, Germaine and Ella for a powwow at Realty Park. He laid a map of Changi General Hospital on the table and they huddled over it. He briefed the team members on their duties for Wednesday August 1. Xaden was to keep an eye on Lina's movements at the detention centre and enroute to the hospital. He could track her location using the GPS embedded in little Busy. He had to text Lina's position on the road every few minutes. They might have to change their plan if the ambulance took her to another hospital instead of Changi General Hospital.

Meanwhile, Kuan Hee, Germaine and Ella would be in Lina's brother's van. Germaine and Ella would enter the A&E Department together and Kuan Hee would station himself near the registration counter. Xaden was to text Kuan Hee the moment the ambulance arrived at the hospital. Germaine and Ella were to distract Lina's escorts so that Kuan Hee could rescue her. He and Lina would leave the A&E Department through the rear exit. They would go to Tampines Avenue five where Lina's brother would station his van. Germaine and Ella would leave the premises together once Kuan Hee and Lina had made their getaway.

"It looks easy on paper," said Kuan Hee. "But, anything can go wrong that morning. That's when you have to act accordingly. Remember—your safety is important."

"Are the escorts armed?" asked Germaine.

"I can't tell for sure," said Kuan Hee. "Just distract their attention. Ask for directions or something like that. The guards can't pull out their gun for no rhyme or reason."

"Won't it be risky for you?" asked Ella.

"They might shoot when Lina and I make a run for it. But, I don't think they will, especially when there are so many people in the A&E Department. They may not want to take a risk."

"I can't park along Tampines Avenue five. It's a busy road," said Lina's brother. "If a traffic policeman sees me, I will have to make a big round to come back to the hospital. So I'll wait on a service road. Once I see you and Lina, I will drive onto the main road."

"OK then. Any questions?" asked Kuan Hee. "Xaden, can you manage on your own?"

"Yes, I can," said Xaden.

"Remember to tell your aunt to act as if she's in terrible pain," said Kuan Hee.

"I will, don't' worry," said Xaden.

"And, remember to get little Busy to fly to the van once your aunt arrives at the hospital," said Kuan Hee. "We can't afford to lose little Busy."

"Yes, Uncle Kuan Hee," said Xaden.

CHAPTER 7

The day of the rescue came. It was a blustery morning. Dark clouds threatened to pour rain over Singapore, but these cleared quickly. The sun remained in hiding behind the clouds most of the time.

Xaden had stationed himself on the open field across the road from the detention centre in Tampines. It was a good day for flying a *layang* here, for the winds were howling away and dishevelling his hair. Xaden ran his fingers through his hair, trying to comb it into place. But it was an impossible task. The next gust sent it into an untidy mob again. He lay prone on the grass near the road; Kuan Hee had told him to be on the alert for lightning strikes, for he was an easy target on the flat open ground. Little Busy flitted unsteadily through the turbulent air towards its destination—the third level of the detention centre. Soon it was hovering over Lina in her holding room.

"Aunt Lina, Uncle Kuan Hee says he will take action at the A&E Department," said Xaden through little Busy's speakers.

"Righto," said Lina. She was in high spirits today; then she remembered the roleplay she had been entrusted to carry out. She furrowed her brows, clutched her stomach as if some tormenting animal was inside it, ready to wreck hell in it. She curled into a ball and sat in a corner, wailing at the top of her voice. She screamed as if she had never screamed before. Her voice echoed through the quiet corridor outside her room.

In seconds, there were heavy footsteps approaching her room. Then the door creaked open, and two female guards appeared. They took turns to try to calm her down, for she was disturbing the otherwise tranquil peace on the level. Clearly exasperated, one suggested taking her to seek medical attention. She was afraid Lina would die under her care; she would have a lot of explaining to do to her superiors. They grabbed Lina's arms and shuffled out of the room with little Busy flying discreetly behind them.

On the open field, Xaden busied himself giving updates of Lina's movements to Kuan Hee who had reached Changi General Hospital in Lina's brother's van together with Germaine and Ella. Lina's brother parked his van in a street behind Changi General Hospital. The street opened into Tampines Avenue five where he would be picking Lina and Kuan Hee. As arranged, Germaine and Ella would leave separately. The team waited in the van; they would attract unnecessary attention if they loitered in the hospital premises.

Little Busy flitted into an ambulance together with Lina and her escorts. It perched itself on a shelf on the side of the ambulance, from where Xaden had a good view of the occupants and the back window of the vehicle. Xaden could monitor the housefly's position using the map on the screen. He reported the ambulance's route to Kuan Hee via his smartphone.

It was some minutes before Kuan Hee could ascertain the destination of the ambulance. It did not leave Tampines. Instead it turned into Tampines Avenue five and was now passing Tampines Swimming Complex. Kuan Hee knew the ambulance was heading for Changi General Hospital. It was now four junctions away from the hospital. Lina's brother gave them the all clear to leave the van. Germaine and Ella left together, followed by Kuan Hee seconds later. The two groups took different routes to the A&E Department on the ground floor. It was difficult for Kuan Hee to avoid the eyes of the two CCTV cameras perched on the walls of the A&E Department. Between them, they covered the entire hall. The cameras could see Germaine and Ella too. It was a risk they had to take. There was no way for them to neutralize the cameras; there were too many eyes in the hall.

Kuan Hee sat among the patients in the corner, near the rear exit. Germaine and Ella had just entered the place. They walked around the hall, pretending to be curious visitors. Suddenly, Kuan Hee sat up; Xaden had texted Lina's arrival at the hospital. He kept his eyes peeled for Lina. The front door rolled back and Lina entered the hall in a wheelchair with a paramedic and two female escorts. *Good. They are not armed,* Kuan Hee told himself. Germaine and Ella had seen them too, and were walking towards them. The paramedic stopped the wheelchair next to a curtained consultation area and gestured one of the escorts to follow him to a counter. Now, Lina was alone with the other escort. At once, Germaine and Ella reprised their act. They pretended to be lost and asked the excort for direction. Kuan Hee took the chance to come behind the three. He grabbed hold of Lina's hand. Together, they sprinted towards the back exit, leaving the three still in conversation. Suddenly, the escort at the counter shouted. She had seen the pair moving towards the exit. The other escort turned and ran towards the pair. Meanwhile, Germaine and Ella quickly made their exit via the front door.

By now, Kuan Hee and Lina were running along the service road behind the hospital. Lina did not dare to look back. The two escorts were no match for the youngsters and the pair was soon on Tampines Avenue five where the van was waiting for them. The side door was open. They jumped into the back of the van and shut the door. The van screeched off. There was no sign of their pursuers.

Lina hugged Kuan Hee tightly. They had not seen each other for nine days; to Lina, it was an eternity. She planted little kisses on Kuan Hee's face.

"Kuan Hee," she cooed. "I'm so glad to see you. Aren't you glad to see me, Kuan Hee?"

"Yes, dear. Of course, I am, dear." Pressing Lina against his side, he continued, "You are much thinner."

"Is that supposed to be good or bad?"

"Why, dear, it's both good and bad—good that you are getting slimmer, and bad that you have not been eating well."

"You are so bad."

"Seriously, I miss you. Huei Huei misses you. So too your mum and family."

"I forgive you, Kuan Hee." She snuggled against him. She had missed the warmth of his body the past week. "You know, I almost became sterile."

"Yes, dear."

"Just imagine. No more children for the rest of our lives."

"I know, dear."

"Where's little Busy?"

"Don't worry. It's perched safely on top of the mirror in the driver's section. Xaden piloted it back here once you entered the hospital."

"Xaden's a good help, isn't he?"

"Yes dear. So too your cousin Germaine and her friend Ella."

"Yes, *hor*. We have good friends."

"Yes, dear."

"Where are we going?"

"Realty Park, dear."

"My uncle's shop?"

"Yes, dear. I've been hiding there the past few days."

"Can I see Huei Huei now? Can we go see her first?"

"Not yet, dear. We need lie low for a while first. Perhaps, later."

"But, I haven't seen my baby, Kuan Hee."

"All in good time, dear."

The smartphone beeped. Xaden had texted Kuan Hee. He was on his way back to Hougang on bus number 72. Then Germaine texted to say both she and Ella were taking an Uber ride home.

Good. Everyone's safe, thought Kuan Hee. After nine days of pouring rain, some sunlight had come into the pair's lives.

But, they were not home free yet. The G operatives were looking for them. They had to be on the run from now on, but for how long? It was a question neither had an answer to.

The van came to a stop behind the shophouse in Realty Park. After unloading its human cargo, the van drove off. Lina's brother was not of many words. In his silence, he showed his concern for his little sister. He knew the pair wanted to be alone; after their ordeal, they surely had a million things to tell each other.

Xaden texted Kuan Hee using his smartphone again. His father was fetching him home so he would not be coming to Realty Park. Kuan Hee knew it wasn't a coincidence; they all meant well.

Kuan Hee and Lina sat huddled on the floor of the small room above the hairdressing salon in Realty Park. They felt the warmth of sunlight coming through the uncurtained glass panels of the window above them. The opposite wall glared in the sun's reflection.

"We are fugitives now, dear."

"We've got to be in hiding always?"

"I'm afraid so. As long as this government is in power."

"I can't go home?"

"It would be dangerous, dear."

"Our Huei Huei? We can't see her?"

"Certainly not, dear. When the situation improves, we will take her back, but in the meantime she needs your mum to take care of her. Perhaps, in a month or two."

"But, it's too long a wait."

"We can video call your mum and watch Huei Huei on the screen."

"We will be staying here forever?"

"Not forever, dear. Maybe, for a few months."

"Kuan Hee, what's wrong with us?"

"Why do you say that, dear?"

"Because we seem to be getting into trouble quite often."

"It's not us. We are OK. It's the country—it's in bad shape. With the wrong leaders, it's going into a tailspin, and there's probably nothing we can do about it."

Then there was a long silence. Kuan Hee was thinking deeply again. Kuan Hee cuddled Lina as she curled up against his body.

"Kuan Hee, shall we…"

"Of course, dear." He knew what she wanted; she didn't have to say it out. The pair spent an intimate afternoon caressing each other and saying sweet nothings. It was a necessary respite from the shocking experiences of the past few days.

That evening, Xaden brought dinner and a message from Lina's mum. Some people from the Ministry of Social Affairs had come to the house. They asked her whether she had seen Lina. They told her Lina had absconded from the transition centre and it was an offence to harbour her.

"That settles it. We can't visit your mum for the time being; they might be watching the flat."

"Can we video call my mum now? I miss Huei Huei. I want to see her."

"Sure, dear. Let me launch the Skype app."

So, though Lina and Kuan Hee were unable to see their little daughter in person, they could watch her live on the screen. It was pure entertainment for the pair, seeing little Huei Huei wriggle on Lina's bed and make grunting sounds. It wasn't a perfect arrangement, but in these difficult times, it was second best.

CHAPTER 8

Brigadier Walmsley was on the walkie-talkie again to update Kuan Hee on the search for his parents.

"Where are the AA batteries we bought yesterday?" asked Kuan Hee.

He replaced the weak batteries with the new ones that Lina handed him.

"Kuan Hee, in a nutshell, we believe your parents are being held in Singapore. Over."

"So it's not the Russians after all? Over."

"We have reason to believe your parents were abducted by elements of the Singapore army. Over."

"Brigadier Walmsley. Why would the Singapore army want to kidnap my parents? They are citizens here. Over."

"Kuan Hee, that's what I want to know too. But our operatives have confirmed that the mole in the research unit led a special unit of the Singapore army to the secret base in Airlie Beach. Our investigations indicate these soldiers were Singapore commandoes in civilian clothes. They took the research staff to the Singapore army camp in Timbuktoo, North-east Australia. From there, your parents and other research staff were bundled on a

52

Singapore airforce transport plane and flown to Singapore. It all happened more than a year ago. Over."

"Brigadier Walmsley, whereabouts are my parents now? Over."

"I have no news presently. But, we learnt the mole is still in Australia. We are confident of ensnaring him soon. Once we have him in custody, we will be able to get to the bottom of the matter. Over."

"Thanks very much for your help, Brigadier Walmsley. Over."

"Now that we are done with the big thing, let's deal with the others. Did you manage to get Lina out of the detention centre? Over."

"Yes, Brigadier Walmsley. In fact, she's here with me now. We rescued her at the A&E Department in Changi General Hospital. Thank goodness, she's in good shape. Over."

"Why, that's good news indeed, Kuan Hee. But, this means both of you are fugitives from the law. It's bad news. Can you two take care of yourselves? Over."

"It will be difficult, but we sure will try hard, Brigadier Walmsley. Over."

"Good. Good. Kuan Hee. I have got to go now. Will get in touch with you again soon. In the meanwhile, keep safe. Over."

"Yes, Brigadier Walmsley. We will. Over."

Turning to Lina, Kuan Hee said, "If the Brigadier says so, then it must be true—Mum and Dad are in Singapore. They have been living here the past year and we didn't even know it."

"What's with the Singapore government? Why are they doing evil things nowadays?"

"I don't know, Lina. I really don't know. Ever since the last election, the Green Party government has been trampling on us ordinary folks. Looks like these people are hungry for something. I can't put my finger on it—not just yet, anyway."

Then Kuan Hee remembered the communication device embedded in his arm. His father had inserted the device in both their arms five years ago so they could communicate using their brainwaves. They didn't need smartphones!

"Why didn't I think of it? I plain forgot. I can communicate with Dad."

But Kuan Hee had forgotten how to activate the device. He paused. He gestured Lina not to interrupt him; he was now deep in thought. He was trying to recall the passcode. After a long while, his face lit up.

"I remember now." He leaned towards Lina and placed a finger over his lips.

"LOGON ALPA."

"Dad, can you hear me? It's me, Kuan Hee."

There was no one speaking in his mind. Try as he could, he could not hear any voices in his mind. His father was not responding. *Is he sleeping?* Kuan Hee thought. *But, it is mid-morning now.*

"Any luck, Kuan Hee?"

"Nope. Let me try again." He was getting exasperated.

"LOGON ALPA."

"Dad. Dad. Answer me, Dad."

Despite several attempts, he could not get through to his father. Then he sat up.

"Oops! I forgot. This thing has a life span of three years. Dad said the internal mechanism would drain its tiny power cell, even though it's in idle state." Kuan Hee sank in the chair. He placed the back of his hand over his forehead.

"What am I to do now?" he lamented.

Lina comforted Kuan Hee. She shared his helplessness.

Only a few days had passed, yet the room above the hairdressing salon was getting to look like home now. It had the little comforts of home. There was now a television set and a portable refrigerator, brought over by Lina's brother. He had also bought a Samsung smartphone for his sister, with a SIM card in his name. Kuan Hee and Lina had bought two foam mattresses, some blankets and pillows from the neighbourhood shops. There was a coffee maker with which they could make their favourite blend of coffee and a small kettle to boil water to drink. Outside there were two pairs of slippers for them to wear when they visited the toilet at the rear of the premises.

CHAPTER 9

It was August 6. Kuan Hee's smartphone was flooded with calls from Tim, Navin and Yeow Xi. They had been released from reservist training and their smartphones were back in their possession. Tim and Navin knew of the Polaris mobile number, but Yeow Xi was clueless. He merely called back to find out who was trying to reach him.

That evening, Tim and Navin visited Kuan Hee at his new home in Realty Park.

"Why have you moved here?" asked Tim. "Fancy giving up living in a semi-detached and downgrading to a one-room accommodation."

"What happened to your iPhone?" asked Navin. "Why are you using the Polaris line?"

"Hey you guys," said Kuan Hee. "One question at a time please. I can't handle so many."

"Tim, please don't tease Kuan Hee," said Lina. "He's in bad shape already. Don't rub salt into his wounds."

"Jiving. Just jiving, Kuan Hee," said Tim. "No hard feelings."

"Not at all," said Kuan Hee. He was used to getting doses of ribbing from his pals.

"Let's toast to our friendship," said Navin.

"Yeah!" they all said in unison.

"I see you guys aren't wearing the wrist tags," said Kuan Hee.

"They removed it when I went to collect my identity card," said Tim. "I was afraid they might leave it on me."

"Luckily for us, they didn't," said Navin.

"What is this about you being on the run?" asked Tim.

"This guy BG David Foo wanted me to assassinate the President," said Kuan Hee. "Instead, I aimed for his shoulder. He escaped death."

"What? So you are the one who tried to take his life. I thought a foreign government was involved," said Tim.

"Yes. After that, I had no choice but to disappear," said Kuan Hee. "I think they are after me now."

"Why would anyone want to kill the President?" asked Navin.

"I can only guess. Perhaps, the President is in someone's way," said Kuan Hee. "So this someone acted to get rid of the thorn in his flesh."

"I thought with Colonel Tee's death, dirty politics had ended," said Tim. "Looks like it's round two happening."

"When will this clamour for power end?" asked Navin.

"One power hungry party goes out and another even more vicious one comes in," said Tim.

"I thought Singapore would be back on the right track with the Green Party in charge," said Kuan Hee. "But, it seems to be descending into dictatorship again. We can't trust the Green Party government."

"Why do you say that?" asked Navin.

"First, they forced non-graduate mothers to go for sterilisation. Then they killed the Police Commissioner and the Chief Justice. Now, they have retired the high court judges and removed all the remaining judges. Just imagine, they are letting computers act as judges."

"Are you sure it's the Green Party government who ordered the killings?" said Navin.

"The Green Party government is definitely behind this. They used us reservist snipers to do their dirty work for them. They want to get rid of me too—to remove the evidence," said Kuan Hee. "These people are merciless. Do you know they killed three of my fellow snipers just like that?" He snapped his fingers in demonstration.

"Who exactly is this 'they' you are talking about?" asked Tim.

"Brigadier General David Foo and his gang," said Kuan Hee. "He drew his gun and shot dead a fellow sniper in front of me for no rhyme or reason."

"That's surreal, Kuan Hee," said Tim.

"But true, I swear," said Kuan Hee. "Never in my life have I seen such disregard for human life. This David Foo is a murderer."

"No one reported him?" said Navin.

"It's all covered up, including the murders of two other reservist snipers. They killed these two snipers simply because they couldn't run to their designated spot in five seconds."

"The devil!" said Tim. "That's cold-blooded murder."

"So that's why you were frantically trying to reach us the past few days," said Tim. "You want us to think of a way to expose this killer."

"Not so *lah*," said Kuan Hee. "I wanted you guys to help rescue Lina." He proceeded to describe how Lina was detained at Kandang Kerbau Hospital and held in detention. He ended with a blow-by-blow account of the rescue at Changi General Hospital.

"Fancy going on an adventure without us two," said Navin.

"I didn't mean to," said Kuan Hee. "I had no choice."

"By the way, congrats!" said Navin. "Boy or girl?"

"It's a girl," said Lina.

"A real pretty princess," said Kuan Hee.

"*Wah*, you two work so fast," said Tim.

"No, *lah*," said Kuan Hee. "It was an accident." He

grinned from ear to ear.

"Kuan Hee, you talk too much," said Lina. "You are drunk."

"Lina, he's not," said Navin. "Look! He's only had two beers. And his face is not flushed."

"No more beers for you," said Lina. She pushed the beer cans towards Navin and Tim.

"There's another thing that I wish to share with you," said Kuan Hee.

"Don't keep us in suspense, *leh*," said Navin. "Out with it, man."

"My mum and dad have been kidnapped," said Kuan Hee.

"What? Not again!" said Tim. "Kuan Hee, your parents are a magnet for kidnappers."

"Be serious, Tim," said Lina.

"Sorry, *lah*," said Tim. "Just jiving again."

"How did it happen?" said Navin. "I thought they are in Australia."

"Brigadier Walmsley, whose organisation my dad works for, told me my parents were kidnapped by Singapore commandoes in Airlie Beach," said Kuan Hee.

"Singapore commandoes?" said Navin. "Are you kidding?"

"Do I look like I'm kidding?" said Kuan Hee.

"Sorry," said Navin. "Why would they do such a thing?"

"My dad is doing top-secret work for the US government," said Kuan Hee. "I reckon the Green Party government wants to get its hands on this top-secret technology."

"I guess they have taken your parents back to Singapore," said Tim.

"That's exactly what I think too," said Kuan Hee. "Brigadier Walmsley is investigating the disappearance. He says he will be getting back to me soon. I forgot to add— the entire research team has been kidnapped."

"If I didn't hear this from you, I mean, if someone else had told me this," said Tim, "I wouldn't believe him. The very idea that our government can be so despicable."

"It took me some time to accept this idea too," said Kuan Hee. "Like I said earlier, I am pretty sure this Green Party government is evil. We have elected the wrong guys into government."

"Count me in," said Tim. He knew what was on Kuan Hee's mind.

"Me too," said Navin.

"Here we go again," exclaimed Tim. *My life is never dull, not with Kuan Hee as my friend,* he told himself.

CHAPTER 10

Brigadier Walmsley had contacted Kuan Hee on the walkie-talkie and told him he wanted to meet up with him. This time, their venue would be ToastBox Café at Plaza Singapura.

"I think the Brigadier has found my parents," said Kuan Hee.

"How do you know?" asked Lina.

"The urgency in his voice," said Kuan Hee.

The Brigadier had not said much, beyond suggesting the meeting place. The pair was seated in the alfresco part of the café, facing the taxi stand. They had arrived early to grab some seats. ToastBox Café outlets were popular with the locals.

The Brigadier waved to them as he walked from the taxi stand. As usual, he was wearing a hunting hat.

"Sorry to keep you waiting," said the Brigadier.

Aside from sporting more wrinkles across his temple, the Brigadier was much the same man that the pair had met five years ago in Hougang Bus Interchange.

"I've grown to like the *kopi oh kosong* at ToastBox," said Brigadier Walmsley, as he stroked his straggly beard. "I must remember to buy some when we leave afterwards."

Even as he was talking, Lina was already on her feet. She went to queue at the counter and returned with two bags of coffee powder. Kuan Hee and the Brigadier were engaging in small talk.

"You know, Kuan Hee," said the Brigadier. "In the late 1970s, Plaza Singapura was a favourite venue for families during the weekends."

"It still is," said Lina.

"Is it?" said the Brigadier. "If my memories serve me right, there was a department store by the name of Yaohan here. It occupied the ground and basement floors. People flocked here to buy groceries and shop for clothes."

"Yes. My dad told me he spent his Saturdays here with his schoolmates," said Kuan Hee. "They would meet at Medo Restaurant, opposite the road, for a Western lunch before hopping over to Plaza Singapura to while away the afternoon."

"Is that so, Kuan Hee?" said the Brigadier. "I used to come here nearly every weekend too. Let me see now. I was based in Sembawang at the time."

It took a while before the Brigadier got down to business. It was his habit to seize up the surroundings first.

"Kuan Hee," said the Brigadier. "In a nutshell, your parents are in Singapore right now."

Kuan Hee and Lina sat at the edge of their seats. They were now listening intently to the Brigadier whose voice had dropped to a whisper.

"Your parents and the other researchers are being held at the Battle Box in Fort Canning Hill," said the Brigadier.

The pair gasped. Fort Canning Hill was a tourist attraction. The Battle Box was where the British military commanders sited their Command Centre in Singapore during the Second World War.

"The Battle Box is merely a stone's throw away from here," said Kuan Hee. "It's—it's—" He was about to point in the direction of the Battle Box when the Brigadier caught his hand and gently placed it on the small table.

"There's no need to draw attention to us," said the Brigadier as a matter-of-factly.

"Sorry, Mr Walmsley," said Kuan Hee. "I got too excited, I guess." By now he had realized the reason for the Brigadier choosing to meet at Plaza Singapura.

"Our sources in Singapore tell us your parents have been held there for the past year," said the Brigadier. "It's now a restricted area, guarded by soldiers around the clock. It would be difficult to mount a rescue."

"Will you help us, Mr Walmsley?" said Kuan Hee.

"You know, Kuan Hee. The last time, we were dealing with a dictator who usurped power in a coup. So we could mobilise the Delta Force. This time it is a democratically elected government in office. My government would think very hard before agreeing to move against a legally installed government. Remember—the United States stand for Life, Liberty and the Pursuit of Happiness. We fought hard for these ideals. We try our best to protect these ideals too. Anywhere in the world."

"But the soldiers kidnapped my parents and the others from your research centre in Australia," said Kuan Hee. "That should be enough reason for the US government to take action."

"Kuan Hee, even though we know this, we can't send our rangers into Fort Canning to rescue them. It's a politically sensitive matter. My hands are tied," said the Brigadier. "You see, after the downfall of the military regime in your country, there were discussions on moving our logistics support group back to Sembawang Naval Base. But this has been put on the backburner by the Green Party government. We need to be careful how we move in this situation."

The Brigadier twiddled his thumbs as he sat in thought. Then he took a sip of coffee and looked in Kuan Hee's eyes.

"I can't carry out a rescue. But, I can provide you with support—equipment, information and backup," said the

Brigadier. He took out a paper bag from his jacket pocket and handed it to Kuan Hee.

"This will be useful to you," said the Brigadier. "Go ahead, open it."

Kuan Hee unfolded the bag and peered inside. It looked like two pairs of glasses. He took them out and held them in his hands. With the coffee cups and cake plates, there was hardly any free space left on the small table. He passed a pair to Lina.

"State-of-the-art technology," said the Brigadier. "Put them on."

"They look like Google Glass eyeglasses," said Lina. "How do I use them? What do I use them for? How do I activate them?"

"Slowly, dear girl," said the Brigadier. "So many questions. How do I answer them all?"

"Sorry, Mr Walmsley," said Kuan Hee. "She just can't contain her excitement."

"These are manufactured by a project at Google Glass. They are in the experimental stage," said the Brigadier. "You can hide your identity by wearing them."

"Hide my identity?" said Kuan Hee.

"Yes. What I mean is—cameras can't identify you. CCTV cameras will see a different you. Try scrolling the different figures you can use. Simply say 'menu', then 'identity choices', then 'OK'."

Kuan Hee and Lina did as instructed and they were treated to a variety of faces, of different races and cultures. They chose one.

"Kuan Hee, you still look the same," quipped Lina.

"You too, Lina," said Kuan Hee.

"My dear children," said the Brigadier. "Only digital devices cannot recognize you. You will still look the same to anyone you meet. Anyway, the good thing is—you can move around unencumbered."

"How does it do that?" asked Lina.

"It projects a chosen face that hugs your face, so digital

devices see only the chosen face. They can only scan that face," said the Brigadier.

"Thank you very much," said the pair in unison.

"It will take a while for you to get used to the features. It's voice activated, you know, like other Google Glass devices. You can google information on Google Glass. These glasses can do all other Google Glass devices can do, and more," said the Brigadier. "You can also use it to contact me, to talk to me. No need to use the walkie-talkie."

"How do I change the battery?" asked Lina.

"These run on solar energy," said the Brigadier. "It's impregnated with solar cells. Also, it uses the Polaris satellite, so no one can track you."

"That's the same carrier that Dad uses," said Kuan Hee.

"I know," said the Brigadier. "I gave him access to Polaris. You know, Polaris is a secret US government spy satellite."

"Is that so?" said Lina. "No wonder, I can't google information on it."

"How do I use it to talk to you?" asked Kuan Hee.

"All the instructions are in the guide in your glasses," said the Brigadier. "Call up the menu and scroll through the options. My number is already listed in the Contacts section. Remember, when I talk to you, only you can hear me, others can't. The device uses bone conduction."

"Bone what?" said Lina.

"Just google 'bone conduction'. You will find all the information you need," said the Brigadier. "This part is not classified information."

CHAPTER 11

It was the second time in a week that the four friends had gathered in the small room above the shophouse in Realty Park. They were here to discuss the rescue of Kuan Hee's parents and the other researchers. Their focus point was the Battle Box, a relic from the Second World War.

"I visited the Battle Box during my secondary school days. It was a museum then," said Kuan Hee.

"I can still recall the layout of the place," said Kuan Hee. He took a piece of blank paper and proceeded to sketch a plan of the underground bunker. He paused now and then, erased some lines and drew new ones. In minutes, the plan was complete. Everyone leaned forward to take a look.

"It's big," said Tim. He counted the number of rooms. "There must be at least twenty rooms."

"There should be more. I can't recall the locations of the other rooms," said Kuan Hee. "So I have not drawn them in."

"Where does this stairwell lead to?" asked Navin.

"The park above the bunker. There is a concrete block protruding above the ground and a metal door on it. Let me google the place," said Kuan Hee. He took out his smartphone and searched for 'battle box' on google.com. Then he clicked on the images tab. Columns of pictures appeared on the screen and he scrolled down the thumbnails of the pictures till he found what he was looking for.

"Here it is," said Kuan Hee. He pointed to the protruding structure in the middle of an open grassy space. He visited thebattlebox.com. It hosted the picture they were viewing.

"Wow! It has everything about the Battle Box," said Lina. "There are many more pictures on this Website."

"Yes, it is a goldmine of information," said Navin. "The museum has been closed for a long time, and yet this Website is still online."

"We are indeed lucky," said Kuan Hee.

"See whether it has a map of the place," said Tim.

"Click on the side menu, Kuan Hee, where it says 'Inside'," said Lina.

The Inside section listed all the different rooms: Fort Commander's Office; Commander, Fixed Defences Room; Orderlies Room; Gun Operations Room; and Escape Route. There was no map of the place.

"Click on Escape Route, Kuan Hee," said Navin.

"According to this Website, the escape route was a closely guarded secret," said Tim. "Here are pictures of the corridor leading to the stairwell. And here is the staircase in the stairwell." He pinched the screen and spread two fingers to enlarge the pictures.

"Kuan Hee, go to Exit," said Lina, pointing to the last item on the sidebar.

On the Exit page were photographs of a pair of metal doors, which fitted snugly against a fern-laced backdrop protruding from a steep slope. On top of this slope was a continuous metre-tall granite wall running parallel to the slope.

"I remember we came out this way after the tour, and sat here eating our lunch," said Kuan Hee, pointing to the wide granite walkway in front of the Battle Box's exit.

"How about the Entrance?" said Tim. "Let's take a look."

The entrance was similar to the exit. Both the entrance and exit were built flush against the two sides of a hill, with a wide walkway running parallel southwards and ending at a roundabout.

"I didn't know there are roundabouts in Singapore," said Lina. "I thought they went the way of the Dodo."

"This one is steeped in history," said Navin. "It's been around since the Second World War, so they won't destroy it."

"What's beyond the roundabout?" asked Lina.

"It's a steep slope with a staircase running down to the road below," said Kuan Hee. "My classmates and I climbed up Fort Canning using it."

"I thought the coach took you there," said Lina.

"Nope. The coach dropped us at the National Museum, a stone's throw away," said Kuan Hee. "After visiting the National Museum, we walked to Fort Canning Park for the Battle Box visit."

"I see," said Lina. "What's this?" Lina was pointing at the Interesting Things tab on the sidebar.

Kuan Hee clicked on the tab. There were pictures of different things which could be found in the Battle Box: old oil drums, oil lamps, jerrycans, helmets, signalling sets—all from the war era.

"What's this?" said Navin, fingering a flat metal plate on the screen.

"It's a manhole cover," said Kuan Hee. There is an underground drainage system running throughout the bunker."

"Mmm. Water goes into the bunker. To prevent flooding of the bunker, they arranged for water to be disposed of using this drainage system," said Tim. "Ingenious. Simply ingenious, the British."

"Hey! That's it. The water goes out of the bunker," said

Navin. "There's another way out of the bunker."

"Yeah. But where?" asked Lina. "It doesn't say anything on the Website."

"Yes, I wonder where," said Kuan Hee. He was now fingering the stubble on his chin. He had forgotten to shave today.

"Who's the owner of the Website?" asked Navin. "Perhaps, we can find out more from him or her."

"Considering the amount of information contained on this Website," said Tim. "This fella must be fond of the Battle Box."

"I agree," said Lina.

"There's no contact information," said Kuan Hee. "It doesn't have a contact form either."

"Go to the About page," said Tim.

"It says 'online since 2010," said Kuan Hee. "It's twenty-five years ago."

"I suggest we do a whois search," said Navin.

"Just a moment," said Kuan Hee. He typed the domain name on the whois search engine.

"The contact number looks fictitious," said Navin. "But the address seems real."

"Block 227A Yishun Street twenty-one, #02-711," said Kuan Hee.

"Now that's a lead," said Navin. "Who's going there?"

"I will," said Kuan Hee.

"Me too," said Lina.

"That's settled then," said Tim. "Give us an update when you are done."

"Let's google the plan of Fort Canning Park," said Navin.

Kuan Hee typed Fort Canning Park in the search box on google.com.

The map that came up in the search results detailed the different landmarks on the hill. But it was difficult for them to view it on the small smartphone screen. They had to squint.

"Here. Click on this link," said Navin.

"*Wah*, it's a heritage site," said Lina. "Look at the nine-pound cannons, the old gates and the memorials."

"What's this large coloured patch?" asked Tim. "Zoom in on the writing, Kuan Hee."

"It says 'Fort Canning Service Reservoir," said Kuan Hee.

"Gee, I didn't know there's a reservoir on this small hill," said Lina.

"The reservoir is so close to the Battle Box," said Navin. "I wonder—maybe the drainage system in the bunker empties into the reservoir."

"Possible," said Tim.

"Shall we go recce the place?" asked Navin. "We need some perspective on the hill."

"Let's wait for Kuan Hee to talk to the Website's owner first," said Tim. "At least, we'll have some direction, instead of feeling around in the dark."

"I agree," said Kuan Hee. "The owner may have intimate knowledge of the bunker that we can put to good use."

CHAPTER 12

"This driverless bus is too slow," said Kuan Hee. "It's almost like crawling from one stop to another."

"It isn't slow," said Lina. "Look! The car alongside it is moving about the same pace. You are just too anxious." She was right. Kuan Hee was eager to get his parents out of the Battle Box; he was getting impatient.

Kuan Hee and Lina were on their way to check out the address given in the domain ownership

The pair alighted at the bus stop in front of the neighbourhood centre. Block 227A was opposite the bus stop. It was a new block towering 25 storeys above the ground. They climbed the stairs to a second-storey unit at the corner of the block.

A fortyish fair-complexioned woman opened the door. The pair learnt she was the daughter of the Website owner.

"My father is not living here," said the lady. Kuan Hee's lips pressed against each other. He had been hoping for positive news.

She scribbled an address on a piece of paper and handed it to Kuan Hee. "He lives alone in a studio apartment. He's frightfully independent for a seventy-seven-year-old man."

"He's that old?" said Lina. She couldn't contain her astonishment. She had been imagining a middle-aged man." Kuan Hee glared at her. They were there to fish for information and such words didn't help.

"Yes, he worked at the Battle Box as a guide in the 1990s," said the lady matter-of-factly. "It's been forty years since."

"Thank you very much," said the pair in unison. Kuan Hee was glad the lady saw no offence in Lina's remark.

"Look for him in the evening," said the lady. "In the day, he likes to move around. You see—my father can't keep still."

"Thanks for the tip," said Kuan Hee. "How shall I address your father?"

"You can call him Mr Hon," said the lady.

The pair bade goodbye to the lady and made their way to the bus stop.

"Where's he living?"

"Surprise! It's Hougang Meadows. It's right opposite Holy Innocents' High School. We can walk there from Realty Park."

"It's so near us and we didn't have an inkling. Are we going there now?"

"Yes, dear." Kuan Hee was one who couldn't wait. Once he had set his mind on doing something, he wouldn't rest till it got done.

On the way back by bus, Kuan Hee kept complaining about the slowness of the bus.

"These driverless buses are a pain in the neck." Kuan Hee was leaning forward again for the return journey. It was a different bus. This was a double-decker and they were seated on the upper deck as usual.

"What to do? There aren't enough workers. It's all because our people are not reproducing themselves in sufficient numbers. Besides, this bus isn't slow. It's just your imagination, Kuan Hee."

Kuan Hee wanted to look up Mr Hon immediately, but

Lina was having hunger pangs. He had no choice; they had to adjourn for lunch first.

After a hurried meal at ToastBox café in the basement of Hougang Mall, the pair walked over to Hougang Meadows. Mr Hon lived on the eighth storey of a twenty-storey HDB apartment block. No one opened the door at his unit. They stood there for a while before Kuan Hee realised Mr Hon was not home. Then he remembered what the lady had told him earlier. They had made the trip in vain.

All was not lost. Mr Hon lived within walking distance of Realty Park. They would return to his flat later in the evening.

It was 6:30 p.m. In the dwindling daylight, Kuan Hee and Lina parked themselves in the void deck of the block of flats opposite Mr Hon's apartment. From there, they had an unhindered view of his flat. It was dark inside. He wasn't home yet.

They saw windows in the block light up one by one. Soon, most of the windows were lit, but Mr Hon's remained in darkness. The pair was getting tired, for they had been craning their necks all evening.

Then they saw his unit light up. Mr Hon was finally home. The pair ran to the lift.

A sprightly, wizened old man opened the door. He welcomed them into his flat. He was not surprised to see them; his daughter had told him of their visit to her place. It was a studio apartment, with a small living room and an adjoining bedroom. The kitchen was slightly bigger than Kuan Hee's pantry at 79 Jalan Naung. A statue of the God of Wealth stood atop a tall thin wooden cabinet facing the front door. There were Coca-Cola paraphernalia displayed in it. A sofa sat adjacent to two armchairs in the living room. A MacBook computer and some books sat on a desk set against one wall.

The pair sat on the sofa while Mr Hon leaned forward

in an armchair next to them.

"What is it about the Battle Box that you two youngsters are keen on knowing?" asked Mr Hon.

"Mr Hon, we are interested in the history of the Battle Box," said Kuan Hee.

"So you must have visited my Website," said Mr Hon.

"Yes, and we learnt quite a bit about the Battle Box," said Kuan Hee. "But, there's no map of the bunker. We don't know the exact layout of the place."

"Forgive me for being brunt, but why are you interested in the Battle Box?" said Mr Hon. "It's an old bunker and is of no use to anyone except historians and tourist guides. You two don't strike me as belonging to either group."

"Mr Hon. The truth is—my parents are being held hostage in the Battle Box. My friends and I want to get them out. We need to know the area well so we can plan a rescue," said Kuan Hee.

"Are these people kidnappers?" asked Mr Hon. "Or do your parents belong to some underworld group?"

"Neither," said Kuan Hee. "My dad is a scientist. He works for the American government. He was kidnapped with my mum and other research staff from Australia. They were flown here and kept in the bunker."

Mr Hon was now stroking his sideburn. He leaned on one arm of the chair and gazed into Kuan Hee's eyes. He seemed to be sizing up Kuan Hee. There was a long silence.

"Kuan Hee, that's your name right?" said Mr Hon.

"Yes, Mr Hon," said Kuan Hee. "And she is my wife, Lina."

"Right," said Mr Hon. He was now running a finger across his chin. "To tell you the truth, your story seems far-fetched. It's not that I don't believe you. It's just that this is our first meeting and I do not know you well."

"Mr Hon, I have no reason to be lying to you," said Kuan Hee.

"Kuan Hee, you said your father was kidnapped in Australia and flown to Singapore," said Mr Hon. "Who kidnapped him?"

"The Singapore government—I mean, the Green Party government," said Kuan Hee. "Dad is working on some top secret project for the American government and our government wants in on it."

"Now, why would our government do something like this? And if they really did, the American government would be able to get your father and the other researchers back," said Mr Hon. "So why involve you and your friends?"

Lina was finding it difficult to keep to her seat. She was now sitting at the edge of the chair. Kuan Hee placed a hand on her lap. He was telling her not to crash his efforts.

"Mr Hon, I am in contact with an American operative who works with my dad. He says that the Green Party government is legally elected so his people can't step in to help," said Kuan Hee.

"But, these researchers are working for them," said Mr Hon. "There's no reason for the Americans to turn a blind eye."

"That's what I thought so," Mr Hon. "But the American operative says the American government doesn't want to antagonize the Singapore government, unless there is proof."

"Proof? Proof of what?" said Mr Hon.

"Proof that the researchers are being held here," said Kuan Hee.

"I thought the Americans have got state-of-the-art equipment. Getting proof is a simple affair for them," said Mr Hon.

"I guess they don't want to be embarrassed—in case the rescue fails, or it turns out the researchers are not in the bunker," said Kuan Hee.

"Then how do you know for sure they are there?" said Mr Hon.

"I don't," said Kuan Hee. "That's why I have come here to see you. I thought you might know a way for us—my friends and I—to get inside the bunker so that we can confirm my parents are in it. The American operative has promised to help us after we have got my parents out."

"Is that so?" said Mr Hon. He pursed his lips in thought. "Let me think."

It was getting late and the pair was getting nowhere with Mr Hon. Instead of giving them the information they so badly needed, he took them on a circuitous path that brought them back to square one.

"Who is this American operative?" asked Mr Hon. "And where in Australia are your father and the other researchers based?"

Kuan Hee paused. He could not decide whether to divulge the Brigadier's name. After all, Mr Hon was a stranger. He wasn't sure he could be trusted. Then he realized both Mr Hon and he had something in common. They were dealing with total strangers, and neither could decide whether to trust the other. He reasoned he had to make the first move to break the barrier.

"Brigadier James Walmsley is his name. He is with the Special Forces. Dad's research unit is based in Airlie Beach, on the Whitsundays Coast in Northern Australia," said Kuan Hee.

Mr Hon jotted down what Kuan Hee had told him. He leaned forward again.

"Tell you what," said Mr Hon. "I'll study this and get back to you. Let me have your phone number."

Kuan Hee had prepared himself for this moment. Unlike Lina, he wasn't at all surprised. He told Mr Hon his mobile number.

"This isn't a local number," said Mr Hon.

"It's a satellite carrier number," said Kuan Hee. "It belongs to my dad."

"Really?" said Mr Hon.

"Yes," said Kuan Hee. "What I have told you is the

truth. My dad is really a scientist. Let me demonstrate one of his inventions." Kuan Hee took out little Busy and opened its remote control panel. At once, little Busy rose and flitted into the air. It flew around Kuan Hee, Lina and Mr Hon.

Kuan Hee showed Mr Hon the screen. It had a live video of the view of the room from the cameras in little Busy's eyes.

It was clear Mr Hon was mesmerized. He had never seen anything so fascinating as little Busy.

"Is this for real?" Mr Hon exclaimed.

Kuan Hee let little Busy land on Mr Hon's arm.

"It's so tiny," said Mr Hon, "and futuristic. I've not seen anything like this before. The technology for miniaturizing this robot is way ahead of the times. It must be top-secret."

With its mission accomplished, little Busy flew back into Kuan Hee's backpack.

"Let me sleep on it," said Mr Hon. "I'll contact you again."

The pair thanked Mr Hon for his time and left his flat. Downstairs, Lina fumed.

"We spent two whole hours for nothing."

"No, *lah*. I think Mr Hon has been convinced. He'll help us."

"Will he? I got the feeling he was merely giving us a merry-go-round."

"I think little Busy worked wonders on him. I think he believes what I said. Like he said, give him some time to think over."

Though Kuan Hee was trying to convince Lina with his words, he himself harboured some doubts.

CHAPTER 13

The four friends met at an open space outside Dhoby Ghaut MRT Station. They had come prepared for an afternoon of fieldwork. Fort Canning Park was atop a small hill and there was plenty of walking and standing under the glare of the hot sun. All adorned caps to shade their faces.

"What's with the glasses?" asked Navin. Kuan Hee and Lina were sporting eyeglasses.

"These aren't eyeglasses," said Kuan Hee. "These are Google Glass devices. They help disguise us."

"You guys still look the same to me," quipped Tim.

"They hide our real faces from the CCTV cameras," said Lina.

"*Wah!* Is that for real?" said Navin. "I didn't know Google Glass eyeglasses have got this capability."

"The eyeglasses work. They really do," said Lina. "Brigadier Walmsley gave these to us. He knows the G operatives are after us."

"Let's move off," said Kuan Hee. "We are drawing curious looks here."

Tim and Navin were tasked to explore the hill on the

reservoir side. So they separated from Kuan Hee and Lina who were to check out the Battle Box. The four friends would rendezvous at the old gate near the Registry of Marriages.

Kuan Hee and Lina walked across Penang Lane, climbed up the steps next to the Park Mall Dragon Fountain, crossed a small road and clambered the long concrete   stairs leading to the roundabout on Fort Canning Hill. As they ascended the last step on the slope, they panted. Lina bent over, pressing her hands on her knees. She looked back down the steep slope.

"We must have climbed more than a hundred steps," she groaned.

"It's actually ninety-three steps," said Kuan Hee, bending down. "I counted them as we moved up the stairs."

"I'm definitely not going down this way afterwards," said Lina.

The pair saw soldiers about fifty metres ahead, in front of a white single-storey rectangular building with a gable roof. The cobbled lanes on both sides of the building were cordoned off with metal barriers. The building had doors facing the roundabout and the left lane. A soldier, armed with a rifle, guarded each of the lanes. It appeared the building was being used as a guardhouse.

"We can't go any further without attracting the sentries' attention. They have got a clear line of sight all the way to the roundabout. This was a tourist area previously; now the area is sealed off."

"Where's the Battle Box?"

"Both lanes lead to the Battle Box. It is about fifty steps from the entrance to the lane. In fact, the bunker is situated underground between the two lanes."

"And the reservoir?"

"The reservoir lies beyond the Battle Box. The Battle Box and reservoir are all in a straight line from here."

Kuan Hee raised his hand directly in front of him and pointed ahead of them.

"We can't even get close to the Battle Box. How are we going to mount a rescue when we can't even see the Battle Box from here?"

"Lina, things don't look too bad. Don't forget—we've got little Busy with us."

"How could I have forgotten about it?"

"Now, we've got to find a cosy place to hide."

The pair made a left turn before the roundabout and followed the winding road. Kuan Hee spied a small open space on the grass behind a clump of bushes. He signalled for Lina to follow him. This spot was in front of a tall Tembusu tree so it provided shade from the hot afternoon sun. They could not see the guardhouse from here, but they had an unobstructed view of the surroundings. It would be easy to make an escape if soldiers chanced upon them. Kuan Hee checked to see the ground was clear of ant routes before the pair settled down on the grass. He didn't want a colony of ants to startle Lina. Kuan Hee placed the remote control for little Busy on his backpack. Little Busy flitted out of the backpack and hovered over them.

Meanwhile Navin had texted Kuan Hee to tell him they had to abort the recce; Fort Canning Park was crawling with soldiers. There was no way for them to observe the area unnoticed. It was too risky. Kuan Hee communicated the pair's location to Navin.

The pair heard the rustling of leaves on grass. It was Tim and Navin. Kuan Hee raised a hand above the bush and the two men joined them behind the bush.

"Did you have better luck here?" asked Tim.

"We couldn't even get near the Battle Box. The old building in front of the roundabout has been turned into a guardhouse. Anyone there can see all the way to the roundabout. There's no way to get past the soldiers undetected," said Kuan Hee.

"We walked around the hill towards the reservoir, but there is a chain-link fence running around the perimeter. There are soldiers patrolling behind the fence. It seems Fort Canning Hill has become a military installation," said Navin.

"How can a tourist attraction become a military camp?" said Lina.

"It's difficult to move around without being spotted by people on the hill. It's an attacker's nightmare."

"Don't forget Fort Canning Hill was originally an army camp hosting the British armed forces. It was purpose-built, with the bunker as a top-secret command centre for the British commanders," said Kuan Hee.

"How are we going to rescue your parents?" asked Tim. "It looks like an impossible task."

"Let's see what little Busy can tell us about this place," said Kuan Hee. He instructed the robot housefly to fly towards the guardhouse.

"Who's taking notes of our findings?" asked Tim.

"Let me do it," said Lina.

As little Busy flew over the guardhouse and up the cobbled lane, the four friends were treated to an aerial view of Fort Canning Park. There was a lone guard outside the entrance to the bunker. Aside from this, there was no one in the open space between the bunker's entrance and the building opposite it.

Little Busy flew over the bunker's entrance, up the slope to a large open park. There was not a soul in sight. The old historical gates and arches adorning the park, accustomed to the fawning attention of photograph snapping tourists, looked out of place in the deserted landscape.

Little Busy flew down the other side of the park onto the exit of the bunker. There was another guard stationed here. The metal doors were shut too. There was no gap through which the robot housefly would use to sneak into the bunker.

At the edge of the granite walkway was a chain-link fence running parallel to it. Beyond it, on the bottom of a steep slope, stood another historical building, now a hotel.

"This slope is the shortest route to the Battle Box," said Tim. "Only the fence stands in the way."

"The galvanized steel mesh is clean of rust. It could not be more than a year old," said Navin.

"Seems this is the easiest and fastest way to get to the bunker," said Kuan Hee.

"So we use this way to escape from the bunker too?" said Navin.

"Anyone disagrees?" asked Kuan Hee. There was silence.

"Now, we have to wait for someone to come out or go inside the bunker," said Navin. He took a puff on a cigarette he had lit. He was an occasional smoker. "It may be a long wait."

"No choice," said Kuan Hee.

"Can we move somewhere else to keep watch?" asked Lina. She was scratching her arms and legs. Then she slapped her face and looked at her hand. "The mosquitoes here are pesky." Kuan Hee had been careful to choose a spot free from ants, but it did not occur to him that Fort Canning Hill was a magnet for mosquitoes. None of the four friends were spared.

"I don't think there is a better place than here. Any nearer and we could be found out," said Kuan Hee. "Besides, the whole hill seems to be infested with mosquitoes. Even if we change to another spot, there is no guarantee it will be mosquito free."

"I agree with Kuan Hee," said Navin. "Anyway, we can always rub some oil over the bites."

"Next time, I will remember to bring some mosquito repellent patches," said Lina.

"Nobody is coming in or out of the bunker," said Navin. "We can't continue waiting like this."

"I saw some round things protruding out of the ground in the park," said Tim. "Can we get little Busy to check them out? Perhaps, it is a way in."

"Where?" asked Kuan Hee. He directed little Busy to fly over the open ground on top of the slope.

"See the metre-long circular tops coming out of the ground?" said Tim. "Get little Busy to fly closer."

"Look like air vents," said Navin. "It's logical for them to be here. The bunker needs ventilation."

"I'll fly little Busy into the—the air vent," said Kuan Hee.

The four pressed their heads closer to the remote control screen. It was dark in the air vent but little Busy's eyes had thermal and infrared imaging sensors. It made short work of moving around in the dark. It was simply amazing how little Busy managed to avoid hitting the walls of the duct. The housefly flitted through a long winding duct, which made several ninety-degree turns before finally ending in a rectangular contraption with louvred openings on one side.

Finally, little Busy peeped through the lourved opening and darted out into the open space. The room, the size of a HDB kitchen, was brightly lit. It had a high ceiling. The contraption occupied nearly half the room. The doorless room opened into a long corridor. LED tubes installed at regular intervals on the ceiling provided illumination for the bunker.

Little Busy hovered in the corridor. It could not decide which direction to explore.

"Turn left, Kuan Hee," said Lina.

Kuan Hee laid the map he had drawn next to the remote control.

"See—the bunker is a rectangular labyrinth of rooms, with the entrance located on one breadth of the rectangle and the exit on one length of the rectangle," said Kuan Hee.

"Where is little Busy now?" asked Lina.

"Here," said Kuan Hee, pointing to a corridor on the map.

Little Busy turned left and flew through the corridor; Kuan Hee moved his finger in unison. There was a fork in the corridor now.

"A left turn will take little Busy past these few rooms and then to the exit," said Kuan Hee. "And a right turn will bring it to the first few rooms at the entrance, which is here."

"Let's see the entrance area first," said Navin. "Find out how they guard the bunker."

Kuan Hee manoeuvred through the passageway towards the entrance.

"There doesn't seem to be anyone around," said Lina.

"They could be in the rooms," said Kuan Hee.

Little Busy was now at the end of the corridor. A metal door stood in front of it. On both sides of little Busy were rooms.

"This door leads to the entrance of the bunker," said Kuan Hee. He remembered being treated to the screams of a loud wailing siren as he and his schoolmates entered the bunker for a visit.

"The left room was the Orderlies Room," said Kuan Hee.

Little Busy flitted into the doorless Orderlies Room. There were two bunk beds, one on each side of the room, and a desk and chair between them. A rifle rack stood next to the doorway. There was hardly any space left for more furniture. No one was in the room.

"Four beds equals four guards," said Tim.

"How do you know they are for guards?" asked Lina.

"See the rifle rack?" said Tim.

"These are for rifles?" said Lina.

84

Tim nodded.

"Why don't we see people in the bunker?" asked Lina. "Where have they all gone?"

"The place seems deserted," said Tim.

"But the thermal sensors on little Busy show the air temperature is twenty-two degrees Centigrade. The air-conditioning is switched on," said Kuan Hee.

"Where could your parents be?" said Navin.

Little Busy flew back through the passageway and turned right this time. It passed room after room but there was no way to enter them—there were no gaps between the metal doors and the floor. It made a left turn and another right turn and the four friends found themselves looking at a metal door at the end of a long corridor.

"It's the exit," said Kuan Hee, pointing to its location on the top of the map.

"Let little Busy go into the room on the left," said Tim.

"Looks like another room for the guards," said Navin.

"There are three bunk beds here," said Lina. "This room is bigger and longer than the other one."

"Six plus four equals ten guards," said Tim.

"This number doesn't include those at the guardhouse and patrolling the grounds," said Navin.

"Must be a platoon of men," said Kuan Hee.

"How many is that?" asked Lina.

"Around forty to fifty men," said Kuan Hee. "Makes sense. This is a sprawling park that the bunker sits under."

"That many?" said Lina.

A metal door cranked open somewhere in the bunker. Then came the shuffling of boots. The sounds echoed through the passageways into little Busy's microphones.

"Someone or some people are here," said Tim. "There's no way to tell how many from the echoes."

"Let little Busy fly towards the entrance," said Navin.

Little Busy made two turns and the four friends saw at least ten people walking through the passageway. There were two soldiers in front and another two at the back of the group. In between them were civilians.

The four friends were now glued to the screen, trying to make out the faces of the civilians.

"That's Dad," said Kuan Hee. He was now pointing at a head on the screen.

"Yes, it sure is Uncle," said Lina. She was used to calling Professor Wang Uncle though the pair was now married.

"I don't see Mum," said Kuan Hee. "She's not in the group."

Kuan Hee did not recognize the other civilians. They could be members of his father's research team.

"There are six civilians here, not counting your dad," said Lina as she jotted down the information in a little notebook in her hand.

Kuan Hee piloted little Busy over the civilians towards his father. The high ceiling was a boon for little Busy; they would not notice it, unless they craned their necks upwards.

Two soldiers led the civilians into the room at the intersection of two passageways, whilst another stationed himself outside the door. The last soldier was now standing at the entrance.

"These soldiers look like regulars," said Kuan Hee.

"Quick! Follow them into the room, Kuan Hee," said Tim.

It was the first, and smaller, of two adjoining rooms. It served as a changing room. The civilians put on a white gown and wrapped a mesh over their heads. Then they wore masks and visors over their faces.

"It used to be the Fortress Commander's Office," said Kuan Hee. "The adjoining room was the Gun Operations Room."

The civilians walked through a doorway into the larger room. As little Busy flitted through the doorway, it flipped and wobbled. Then it stabilized itself.

"There seems to be turbulence in the air. There is an invisible curtain of some kind of air particles bombarding the doorway continuously," said Tim.

"I think there is a decontamination zone at the doorway," said Kuan Hee. "The larger room must be a clean room."

There was equipment everywhere in the larger room. It was bigger than a classroom. Computer monitors sat on metal racks positioned against one wall. On the other walls, several server cabinets housed a multitude of servers with cables running behind them and trailing across the length of the room. It looked like a mainframe computer room, except there wasn't a platform for cables to run under.

"This must be the brain centre of the bunker," said Navin.

In one section, there were robotic assemblers and next to them, a big piece of equipment, the size of a dining table. On one side was a label: DNA Molecular Assembly. Alongside was a big rectangular box on a stand. It had a pair of rubberized openings through which one could insert one's hands. Inside the box was an array of tubes and capsules on a rack. At the far end of the room was a floor-to-ceiling glass partition. Behind the door on the partition was what seemed to be a small operating theatre.

"Looks like a cloning laboratory," said Tim. Like Kuan Hee, he had majored in nano-technology at Temasek University and was familiar with some of the equipment.

"Yes, indeed," said Kuan Hee. "The walls between the Gun Operations Room and the two rooms beyond have been torn down. So this room is now triple its original length."

A lone soldier was watching over the civilians in the room. The other was resting in the changing room. They were taking turns to keep watch over the civilians.

"The only way in and out is through the changing room," said Navin. "The other doors have been sealed shut."

Professor Wang was now seated at a desk with two assistants flanking him. He was pointing at the computer monitor in front of him and talking to his assistants. He had not noticed little Busy perched on the wall in front of him.

"Looks like the whole bunker has been stripped bare of the museum props," said Kuan Hee. "The mannequins, old telephone exchange, surrender chamber furniture and the large platform on which stood a map of Malaya and Singapore are all gone."

"The bunker is now a bona fide research centre," said Tim. He pointed at the screen. Professor Wang was moving towards the computer servers. He was alone. Little Busy launched itself into the air and flitted towards the professor. It was now hovering over his left ear.

Kuan Hee tapped the microphone icon on the remote control. He slid the volume lever to low.

"Dad. Dad, it's me Kuan Hee," said Kuan Hee.

Professor Wang turned his head. Although the visor and mask hid his face, the corners of his mouth had turned upwards, and his cheeks peaked. He was beaming. He looked behind him. The other researchers were engrossed in their work and the guard was staring blankly into space.

Using a finger, Professor Wang scribbled 'Hi' on the flap of the server rack in front of him.

"Where's Mum?" asked Kuan Hee.

The professor drew a rectangle and a smaller rectangle on its upper right. Then he scribbled an arrow and 'Exit'.

Lina pointed to the rooms next to the exit. "Uncle means Auntie is in one of these rooms," she said.

"It's good Mum and Dad are safe," said Kuan Hee.

Kuan Hee didn't have time to ask more questions, for the professor's assistants were now approaching him.

"Shall we leave little Busy with Uncle?" asked Lina.

"Yes, of course," said Kuan Hee. He directed little Busy to fly under his father's lab coat. It attached itself to his trouser pocket.

"Time to leave the hill," said Kuan Hee. "Our work's done for today."

The other friends were glad to leave Fort Canning Hill. The mosquitoes had been feasting on their blood the whole afternoon.

CHAPTER 14

Sitting at a table next to the glass windows of the food court on the third level of Marina Square, the four friends had a panoramic view of the Marina Bay area. The spiky edges of the 'durians', the nickname for the Esplanade Theatre, cut a stark contrast with the clear blue sky.

"Hey, Kuan Hee," said Navin. "You can remove these glasses now. They look funny on you."

"I simply dread these CCTV cameras," said Kuan Hee, taking off the Google Glass.

"These cameras have been around for ages," said Navin. "But I didn't hear you complain about them before."

"That's because I wasn't being targeted then," said Kuan Hee. "Now, that the G operatives are looking for me, these cameras have become a nuisance. I had to keep avoiding them all the time."

"Not anymore, right?" said Tim. "You have the Google Glass."

"Yes, thank goodness for it," said Kuan Hee.

"The network of connected CCTV cameras in public areas came about because of the terrorist threat in the 2010s. Remember the terrorist attacks in Europe?" said Tim.

"It was good for the purpose then. The world was on edge. We were continually looking over our shoulders, dreading an attack in the streets," said Kuan Hee. "But that's the past. Now this network is letting the G keep watch over us ordinary citizens. It's a double-edged sword. Under a good government, this network was put to good use. But, now under the Green Party government, it's being exploited. That's bad. We have no privacy anymore. Just imagine—they are all over the place. At the MRT stations, bus stops, on the trains and buses, in taxis, along roads, outside shopping malls, walkways, HDB void decks and lift lobbies. They seem to be everywhere."

"Now that you mention them," said Tim. "I agree, they are a pain in the neck." He looked around the food court. "There are CCTV cameras on the pillars here too."

"But these aren't linked to some central monitoring station," said Kuan Hee. "Unlike those in public areas and HDB estates."

"The whole Marina area is swarming with people. There are many soldiers and policemen everywhere we go," said Lina.

"It's the NDP parade, Lina," said Tim.

"Oh, gosh! Today's National Day," said Lina.

"You mean, you didn't know?" said Tim.

"Tim, stop teasing her," said Kuan Hee. "I too forgot today's the big day. Too many things on our minds, you know."

"Sorry," said Tim. "I forgot. It's your parents you are worried about."

"So can we discuss the rescue now?" said Navin. "We've had our fill. Now's a good time to get down to business."

"Remember to keep our voices down," said Tim. "This is a public place."

Kuan Hee unfolded the map that he had sketched and an online map of Fort Canning Hill he had printed. He laid them alongside each other on the large round table. The four friends leaned forward to take a closer look.

"This is where Navin and I explored," said Tim. He fingered a rectangular patch on the map. "That's the reservoir—it sits on Fort Canning Hill. We can't get near the area. There's a chain link fence running around the hill, just after the slope. There are cables on the fence. I believe the fence is electrified."

"The area we recced is farther away from the Battle Box. The shortest route to the Battle Box seems to be where the exit to the bunker is," said Navin.

"I agree," said Kuan Hee. With a finger, he drew a line from the bunker's exit to the hotel down the slope from the hill. "This is the shortest way to the Battle Box."

"Problem is—how to get your parents and the other researchers to go down the slope safely," said Tim. "It's quite steep, you know. And there are only three of us."

"Four," snapped Lina. "You forgot to count me in."

"Sorry," said Tim. "I was talking about muscle power, Lina."

"Let's look at other options," said Kuan Hee. "There are three ways out of the bunker—entrance, exit and the opening on top of the bunker in the open space."

"Are there any secret openings?" asked Lina. "I'm sure they have some means of escape, just in case an enemy attacks."

"According to Mr Hon's Website, the opening on top of the bunker is the secret means of escape. It said only the top brass knew of this escape route," said Kuan Hee.

"How can it be?" said Navin. "The door is in plain sight of everyone in the open space in the park."

"Beats me," said Kuan Hee. "But it was in the past. Perhaps, the open space was a restricted area too. It's difficult to tell now."

"Perhaps, we can ask Mr Hon," said Lina.

"If he agrees to meet us again," said Kuan Hee.

"Hasn't he got back to you yet?" asked Tim. Kuan Hee shook his head.

"These options," said Navin, "aren't good ones. All are equally difficult to use to mount a rescue. I mean, if there are snipers around, we'd be dead meat when we run out of the bunker."

"We still have to choose one," said Tim. "I reckon the exit is the best choice. We can do a diversion, to give time for your parents and the others to escape."

"It seems to be the only option," said Navin.

"Agree," said Kuan Hee. "What about firepower?"

Tim looked around the food court. "We still have the SAR21s and the SSG69 that I have hidden," said Tim in a low voice. "Three SAR21s with one hundred cartridges, and one Steyr SSG 69 with two magazines of five rounds each."

"The last time, I fired one round at Colonel Tee," said Kuan Hee. "So there should be nine cartridges left."

"Tim, I thought you were supposed to return the weapons to the reserve store," said Lina.

"Well, my friends didn't ask for them," said Tim, "and I sort of dragged my feet."

"In a way, it's fortuitous," said Kuan Hee. "We don't have to hunt for weapons."

"These rifles may not be enough to stave off a platoon of soldiers," said Navin.

"Don't forget we have AleXander the robots," said Kuan Hee. "Together, they have enough firepower to take down the bunker."

"You must be joking," said Navin. "The bunker was built to withstand bombs dropped from airplanes, you know."

"Alright," said Kuan Hee. "But the two robots can do big-time damage to a tank."

"I agree," said Navin.

"A surprise rescue just below dawn, when everyone is still in dreamland—that will be the best bet," said Kuan Hee.

"But how will we know where your parents are being held at night?" said Lina.

"Don't forget, I left little Busy behind," said Kuan Hee.

"So we have to be on the hill again to monitor your

parents," said Lina.

"Yes," said Kuan Hee. "We need more information on Mum and Dad—when they sleep, where they sleep, also where the guards keep watch, when the guards change shift."

"Have we forgotten anything?" asked Navin.

Just then there was a commotion in the food court near the entrance. Someone was shouting something. He was pointing to where the four friends were seated. They could not make out what the man was saying; they were too far away. But, it was clear the patrons of the food court were affected. Some left the place hastily.

Tim stood up to look outside the glass windows. The balcony next to the windows blocked his view of the road.

"Something must be happening outside," said Tim. "Shall we go take a look?"

They got up and left the food court. As they passed the cashier's counter, they heard the staff talking about people being killed.

"Let's quicken our paces," said Navin. "I'm curious."

There was hurried activity in Marina Square Shopping Mall. Shoppers were making a beeway for the exits. The four friends followed the crowd and found themselves at the outdoor piazza along Raffles Avenue. It was jampacked with people. Many were taking videos of the happenings in front of them. The crowd spilled into the street.

It was mayhem in the street. There was an unruly mob attacking stalled buses at the bus stop in front of the Esplanade Theatre. There were more than a hundred of them. Soldiers were pouring in from the nearby grandstand where The Float@Marina stood. They had their rifles readied for action. On the road, placards, banners and wooden poles were strewn. Five people were sprawled on the ground. There was blood on them. Some people were helping their fallen friends. Puddles of blood were seen on the tarmac.

Then there was an explosion. The empty buses were being set on fire. The raging fire spread to the bus shelter and soon the bus shelter was but a charred skeleton of itself.

There was a standoff between the mob and the soldiers who had formed a human chain across Raffles Avenue. The soldiers were determined not to let the mob move near the grandstand where the Prime Minister and his ministers were watching the National Day Parade.

But the mob was not made up of burly drunken men. Instead, these were ordinary men and women—office workers, students and passers-by. They were all locals. Some of them were carrying placards reading 'Dump the Green Party', 'No justice, no peace' and 'Return democracy to the people'. Some held caricatures of the Prime Minister showing him with the devil's horns growing out of his head. Others were waving their arms in the air. Some were clapping. They were all chanting 'No one likes the Green Party; remove dictator Ong Chwee Seng' in unison. These were protesters who had turned unruly. Their fellow protesters had been shot and they were now emboldened by anger.

The protesters charged at the soldiers. Then some of them fell in the volley of shots that rang out. The soldiers meant business. They had not qualms about using their rifles. These were regulars, not NSmen. There were screams in the air. The protesters helped their injured comrades and made a retreat. They were sitting ducks against the might of bullets.

Lina pressed her face onto Kuan Hee's chest. He wrapped his arm around her. She was squeamish. She could not take bloodshed. This was Singapore. It could not be happening again—the ruthlessness of the Colonel Tee regime was repeating itself here, five years after the downfall of the regime. For the four friends, it was a nightmare revisited. For Singapore, it was a return to dark times.

"This is insane," said Kuan Hee. "We're killing our own people again." The other friends could not hear him above the cacophony of noises in their surroundings.

Some in the crowd on the outdoor piazza moved into the street. They were disgusted with the soldiers' behavior and were lending their support to the protesters.

By now, the soldiers had erected barricades next to the grandstand. Two soldiers in white ceremonial uniforms were giving orders to some soldiers.

"Must be generals," said Tim. "These two are wearing peak caps with golden embellishments on them. They are too far away for me to make out their ranks."

The cranking of metal wheels on rolling tracks could be heard in the distance. The rumbling became louder as the tops of armored personnel carriers came into view behind the chain of soldiers. The military commanders had summoned help. These heavy vehicles were all spiffed up for ceremonial use. There was not a grain of sand in their tracks. They were diverted to deal with the protesters.

Meanwhile, policemen on duty along the road kept a safe distance from both protesters and soldiers. They were supposed to keep law and order but appeared undecided whose law to uphold—military or civil.

There was a strong stench of irony in the air above the four friends. On the side of the grandstand facing Raffles Avenue, bystanders were treated to a horrific display of the army's ruthlessness. On the other side facing placid Marina Bay, the audience was in a rapturous mood, clapping away and cheering the military parade marking Singapore's National Day. Such was the stark contrast on a supposedly joyous occasion.

Were the invited guests at the grandstand oblivious to the killings taking place in the street behind them? In this day and age of social media, with video postings of the soldiers' ruthlessness going viral, it was unlikely the audience was in the dark. If the guests turned a blind eye to the morbid happenings, it was because they had hidden their conscience behind their fear.

Online forums and editorials condemned the Green Party for its ruthlessness. Articles poured scorn on Prime Minister Ong Chwee Seng for his hypocrisy. He had rooted for the masses during the Tee regime. They thought he was one of them. Now that he had amassed power, he had discarded his Mr Good Guy disguises and shown his true colours finally.

At a command from one of the white-uniformed officers, the armored personnel carriers roared into action. The line of soldiers disintegrated behind the armored personnel carriers, which moved into the path of the protesters. It was a standoff. Either the protesters ran helter-skelter or they would be crushed into smithereens. Just who would blink first? There were just seconds to decide. The armored carriers were menacingly close to the protesters.

In the end, the protesters caved in. They did not have the mettle to stare the raw strength of heavy metal in the face. They screamed their lungs out. They ran as if they had never run before. The armored personnel carriers cleared the road of protesters in no time.

It was now time for the ambulances to do their work. Paramedics attended to the injured and sent them to hospital. The crowd of protesters and spectators disappeared into the surrounding roads and shopping complexes. What were left were soldiers and armored personnel carriers.

The four friends saw firsthand the army's callous disregard for human life.

"Today's happenings show clearly the need for civilian control over the armed forces," said Tim.

"But we have a civilian Prime Minister and

government," said Navin.

"They are only civilian in looks. Definitely military in behaviour," said Kuan Hee. "This PM brooks no dissent."

"It's surreal," said Navin. Images of the burning buses and fallen protesters were fresh in his mind. "I thought such things only happen in movies."

"But it happened once—in Little India in the 2010s," said Navin.

Tim browsed through reports on online news media. "It says on one Website it started as a peaceful protest," Tim said. "Tan Eng Chai got his supporters together to hijack the National Day celebrations at The Float@Marina. The protesters couldn't get past the soldiers so they picked Raffles Avenue to stage their protest."

"Tan Eng Chai, isn't he the secretary general of the Unity Party?" asked Lina.

"Right, Lina. Anything happened to him?" asked Kuan Hee.

"He isn't among those injured," said Tim.

"This editorial on a blog I am reading says we should unite to put the tyrannical government out of business," said Navin.

"Singaporehappenings.com castigates Members of Parliament for turning a blind eye to injustice and murder," said Kuan Hee.

"Wait! Here's breaking news on channelsingapore.com. Minister for Transport Ngoh Shi Ping has resigned. He has pulled out of the Green Party together with a group of MPs," said Navin.

"Did it say how many?" asked Kuan Hee.

"Let me see—twenty-three Green Party MPs," said Navin.

"That means by-elections for the parliamentary seats they vacated," said Kuan Hee. "There is hope, yet. Maybe the Green Party won't have a two-third majority after all. Then they won't be able to pass laws at their whim and fancy after all."

"Ngoh Shi Ping—the veteran politician?" said Tim. "Good *lah*. He's a respected guy. He's popular too."

"So was Ong Chwee Seng, his comrade at the Green Party," said Kuan Hee. "Look what has happened. He did an about-turn after he became PM."

"At least Ngoh Shi Ping is doing the right thing now," said Tim.

"Any other news?" asked Lina.

"The Website of local newspaper The Singapore Tribune reports 'Army crushes demonstration, arrests protest leaders'," said Kuan Hee.

"Is Tan Eng Chai among them?" asked Tim.

"Nope, but some Unity Party members are," said Kuan Hee.

"Where are the other political parties?" asked Navin.

"Search me," said Tim. "Perhaps they can't work together."

"With a common enemy," said Kuan Hee, "they should bury their differences."

"For the good of the country, they should," said Lina.

"It's early days yet," said Tim. "Give them some time to work things out."

"Shouldn't we join in the protests?" asked Navin.

"We should, shouldn't we?" said Lina.

"Of course, we should," said Kuan Hee, "but not yet. Let's get my parents out first."

"Kuan Hee, Are you going back to work at Temasek University?" asked Navin.

"Pretty soon," said Kuan Hee.

"Won't it be dangerous?" said Tim. "The army might be looking for you. You went AWOL, you know."

"Correction. They wanted me to commit treason. I merely tagged along with them," said Kuan Hee. "So if they dare look for me, I will blare out everything."

"You mean you are confident they won't do a thing to

you?" said Navin.

"Er. I think so, *lah*," said Kuan Hee. "Let me try going back to work first. If I smell something wrong, I will scram."

"They may send people to silence you," said Tim. "You know, like this." He slid his hand across his throat in demonstration.

"Aw, Tim. You are horrid," said Lina. She folded her arm over Kuan Hee's and leaned against him.

"Don't frighten the little girl," said Navin.

"Yeah, Tim. You sure are brunt," said Kuan Hee. "But it's possible they will come after me. Just have to be careful."

"Then don't go back to work," said Lina. "I'm afraid, Kuan Hee."

"I am too," said Kuan Hee. "I can't foretell the future. In the meantime, I have applied for a week's leave to cover my absence this week, but I don't have much leave left. So we must get my parents out pretty soon."

CHAPTER 15

Kuan Hee and Lina were watching little Huei Huei on the Samsung smartphone. It was strange that these two newly minted parents had yet to see their daughter in person. Only Lina had held little Huei Huei in her arms, but that was only for a minute or so after she was delivered in the maternity ward.

"Kuan Hee," said Lina. "I miss Huei Huei. I miss her so."

"Me too, dear," said Kuan Hee.

"Shall I ask my mum to bring her here?" said Lina.

"Not a good idea," said Kuan Hee. "She can't be exposed to airborne germs in the open air yet. Her immune system isn't stable yet. It will be bad for her health."

"You mean we have to wait two whole months?" said Lina.

"That's what your mum said, remember?" said Kuan Hee. "Wait at least one more month, dear, OK?"

Kuan Hee's smartphone rang. It was Mr Hon. He wanted to see Kuan Hee.

"He's changed his mind," said Lina.

"I think so," said Kuan Hee. "I hope so." The chat

over the telephone was brief; it was just long enough to set an appointment.

"Mr Hon, what made you change your mind?" asked Kuan Hee. He was in Mr Hon's living room with Lina, Tim and Navin. They wanted to tag along and Mr Hon agreed with the idea. The room was uncomfortably small, but the four friends didn't mind. They were eager to learn everything about the Battle Box from an old hand like Mr Hon.

"I was born in difficult times in Singapore. I lived through riots and curfews, strikes and strife," said Mr Hon. "Then a new government came in and I saw progress and prosperity. Now this fragile thing called peace that I have been accustomed to for most of my life is under threat. Not from a foreign source, but from within Singapore."

Mr Hon paused. With a finger, he stroked his eyebrow.

"What the soldiers did to the protesters in Marina Bay is incomprehensible," said Mr Hon. "This Green Party government is indeed ruthless."

He looked Kuan Hee in the eyes. "I'm sorry I doubted you," he said.

"It's all right," said Kuan Hee.

"Enough digression. Let's talk about the Battle Box," said Mr Hon. "I worked there as a guide for many years. Though it was an old place, it held fond memories for many, many people—from all over the world. The British and Australians visited the bunker the most, for they had fathers or grandfathers who fought the war here in Singapore. They came to honour these people."

Mr Hon paused to take a sip of tea. The four friends flashed awkward smiles at one another. They wondered when he would get around to telling them what they wanted to know. They knew it was pointless to hurry him. Then Mr Hon flipped open a large album yellowed by age and pointed to some photographs.

"These tourists brought not only their memories of

their loved ones, they also gave me some keepsakes left behind by their fathers or grandfathers. They wanted me to share these with other visitors to the bunker. I received letters, ration cards, photographs, etc."

By now, Kuan Hee and Tim were getting fidgety. Navin and Lina were not as impatient as the other two. *Could it be Mr Hon is trying to test them?* Lina wondered. *But why would he want to do such a thing?*

"I'm sorry I am digressing again," said Mr Hon. "It's old age, I guess. Memories are all the more important in our twilight years. But the last point I made earlier is important. A visitor from the United Kingdom passed me something her father had left behind. She came to see the place her father had worked in during the war years."

"You mean her father worked in the Battle Box?" said Kuan Hee.

"Incredulous that this sounds," said Mr Hon, "it is indeed true. She handed me a map of the bunker."

The visitors sat up. They were now all ears. It was the moment they had been waiting for.

Mr Hon turned the pages of the album and stopped at one. He pushed the album nearer to the visitors. They leaned forward. It was a map of the Battle Box drawn in ink on parchment paper. Evidently the map had been folded and then stored for a long time, for the parts of the map along the folds were unreadable. The ravages of time and the tropical weather had taken its toll on the paper. Still, it was possible to make out pertinent information on the map.

Mr Hon tapped his finger on a spot on the map. "See this dotted line running from here to the reservoir?" said Mr Hon. They nodded in agreement.

"It's a secret escape route from the Battle Box," said Mr Hon.

"But I thought the secret escape route was this stairwell leading up to the door on top—where the park is," said Kuan Hee, pointing to the passageway next to the stairwell on the map.

"That's a cock-and-bull story. The real escape route is this tunnel that goes under the bunker," said Mr Hon.

At this point, his visitors were gawking at him. *A secret escape route Mr Hon described on his Website is not a real secret escape route,* they thought in unison. *Why on earth would he want to mislead people?*

"But we got the information from your Website, Mr Hon," said Kuan Hee.

"Why did you mislead people, Mr Hon?" asked Lina. Immediately, Kuan Hee nudged her knee.

"Don't mind Lina, Mr Hon." said Kuan Hee. "She likes to say the wrong things at the wrong time." He didn't want Mr Hon to throw them out of his flat—not when they were so close to finding a secret way into the bunker. Lina pouted her lips. She stared at Kuan Hee but said nothing.

Mr Hon's bushy eyebrows almost met as he glared at Lina. He was not pleased with the way Lina had phrased the question.

"Young girl, I did put the information on my Website," said Mr Hon. "But I didn't mislead people. I told them exactly what the British were telling everyone in their time. I couldn't very well state the truth right? It's a secret tunnel after all."

"Tell us about the secret tunnel, Mr Hon," said Navin. He was anxious to move the conversation away from a confrontation.

"Yes, Mr Hon," said Tim. "Where does it open into the bunker?"

"Oh yes, I was about to get to that when I was rudely interrupted," said Mr Hon. "You see this spot marked 'X' on the map? The tunnel stops here, in the passageway outside the Fort Commander's Office. Here, there is a manhole reaching into the drainage system for the bunker. Open the drain cover and jump inside. The tunnel is three feet wide and two feet deep from here all the way to here."

"Who's taking notes?" asked Tim.

Lina raised her hand. She started scribbling on a small notepad. *Good, this will keep her occupied,* Kuan Hee thought. *She won't have time to think of awkward questions for Mr Hon to answer.*

"The tunnel at this point is wide enough for one person to move through. But it is not deep enough so you have to crawl your way in it," said Mr Hon.

"Mr Hon, how do we get into the tunnel from outside the bunker?" asked Kuan Hee.

Mr Hon fingered a spot marked with a cannon symbol on the map. "Let's see, this nine-pound cannon about a hundred feet away from the bunker is where you enter the tunnel," said Mr Hon. Then he looked through another album and pointed to a picture of an old cannon.

"See this low wall next to the cannon?" said Mr Hon. "Right under the barrel of the cannon, about six feet away, is a hatch opening. You can't see it. You have to dig apart the soil, but it's there all right. It's big enough for one person to jump in, but you have to bend a little for a couple of feet. It opens into a small room just below the cannon. You guys follow me?"

"Yes, Mr Hon," the four friends collectively answered.

"Good. It looks like a dead end, but actually isn't," said Mr Hon. "On the wall, you will see a metal wheel with eight spokes."

"Do we turn the wheel?" asked Navin.

"No, no," said Mr Hon. "Listen carefully. At the end of each spoke you will see an emblem. There are eight different emblems. Look for the golden fish and the parasol. Use your strength. Press them hard simultaneously and kept them depressed until a door opens on the wall next to the wheel."

"Lina, are you taking everything down?" asked Tim.

"Yes, of course," said Lina. "Mr Hon, what are the other emblems?"

"Let me see now, there is a lotus flower, an endless knot, treasure vase, banner, conch, and—what have I missed now—oh yes, a wheel. Gosh, how did I forget the wheel?" said Mr Hon. He opened his fingers one by one as he counted the eight emblems aloud.

"Can all the emblems be depressed?" asked Navin.

"Yes, they can," said Mr Hon. "But they don't do anything for you."

"Mr Hon, how did you know about the emblems?" asked Tim.

"It took me many months," said Mr Hon. "I was working there and, after work, I would try my luck. It needed a lot of brainwork, but it was worth it."

The four friends didn't know Mr Hon was so clever. They were impressed. He was indeed some investigator.

"I was younger then. I thought there was treasure in the secret tunnel—the Yamashita treasure, you know. The thought of finding treasure kept me going," said Mr Hon. "Alas, it was not to be. It was all an illusion. But, all was not lost. I found the secret of the Battle Box. It was a great achievement."

"Yes, Mr Hon, indeed you have," the four friends chorused in unison. He had digressed again, but they didn't mind this time.

"Where did I stop? Yes. Go down the steps into a bigger tunnel. It's a passageway. It's about six feet wide and tall enough for you to walk without having to bend," said Mr Hon. It actually goes on for about a hundred feet until you reach this place." Mr Hon pointed to the manhole marked 'X' on the map.

"There you have it, the secret tunnel," said Mr Hon. He was beaming. He seemed pleased with himself.

"Mr Hon, it was clever of you to find a way in from the cannon," said Lina. She was saying something right this time. Mr Hon's eyes were gleaming; he had forgotten her earlier snide remark.

"Any questions?" said Mr Hon.

"Mr Hon, isn't it dangerous having a tunnel in a hill?" asked Lina. "I mean, won't it collapse if the soil erodes?"

"Dear girl," said Mr Hon. "I was waiting for someone to ask this question. The whole hill sits on a limestone boulder bed. The foundation is, as they say, 'as solid as a rock'. The tunnel will never collapse."

"Mr Hon, you mean the secret passageway goes straight to the manhole at this spot?" asked Tim.

"Oops! I must have forgotten to tell you guys about the contraption near the manhole," said Mr Hon.

"Is there another secret contraption to access to get into the bunker?" asked Kuan Hee.

"Yes. It is another wheel, similar to the one at the cannon," said Mr Hon. "It's at the end of the tunnel; you will see it on the wall. Press hard on the same two emblems. The door on the wall will slide open. Go through it and you will find yourself in the drainage tunnel, about six feet away from the manhole."

"Will the door shut automatically?" asked Kuan Hee.

"It remains open until you shut it," said Mr Hon.

"What if it is shut and I am in the drainage tunnel? How do I get into the tunnel?" asked Kuan Hee.

"On the other side, that is, in the drainage tunnel, there is a similar wheel. Press on the same emblems," said Mr Hon.

"So, Mr Hon, you are saying that at both ends of the tunnel, on both sides of the wall, there is a wheel that controls the door," said Kuan Hee. "And all the wheels operate using the same emblems—golden fish and parasol."

"Correct, Kuan Hee," said Mr Hon. "You catch on quite fast, young man," said Mr Hon.

"Mr Hon, what if the drainage tunnel has got water in it? Doesn't it mean that when we open the door, the water will come rushing in, and the tunnel will be flooded?" said Navin.

"So you finally opened your mouth," said Mr Hon. Navin flashed a grin.

"As far as I know, the drainage tunnel has never been

flooded with water. The water level in the drainage tunnel rises till it is flush with the small drain—about a foot wide and six inches deep. So if you are in the drainage tunnel, you won't get your feet wet. Unless, of course, you happen to step into the small drain, which won't happen unless you are clumsy, of course."

"Thanks, Mr Hon," said Navin.

"So you thought you might be drowned if you went into the tunnel, right, dear boy?" said Mr Hon. Navin grinned sheepishly.

"The tunnel's actually quite safe," said Mr Hon. "I worked at the Battle Box for a little over twenty five years. I had never seen the drainage tunnel flooded."

"Guys, any more questions for Mr Hon?" said Kuan Hee. There was silence in the room. "Mr Hon, I guess that's all the questions we have right now. Can I call you if we should need more information?"

"Sure, you can, Kuan Hee," said Mr Hon. "Always glad to help. But it is very dangerous what you want to do. Do be careful. These army chaps aren't to be trifled with. You may lose your lives."

"Mr Hon, we'll be very careful," said Kuan Hee. "Don't worry, we'll take good care of ourselves, won't we?"

The other three nodded in agreement.

CHAPTER 16

The four friends were at the bottom of Fort Canning Hill, standing next to the Gothic Gate on Canning Rise. They were here to recce the place and plan their moves for the rescue of Kuan Hee's parents.

"These steps lead up the slope to the nine-pound cannon," said Tim. "It's about three minutes' climb from here."

"We can park the getaway vehicle here," said Navin. "There aren't any cameras in the area, except at the Registry of Marriages over on the left. It's a hundred metres away so any cameras there can't see us here."

"The chain link fencing runs parallel to the road on top, all the way from the reservoir on the left to the Fort Canning Centre on the right," said Navin.

"The fence starts right after the cannon, along the low wall," said Tim. "Where did Mr Hon say the hatch is?"

Lina glanced through her notes. "On the ground, about five feet away from the low wall. The cannon barrel points the way," she said.

"Let's go up the slope," said Kuan Hee. "Be on the lookout for soldiers up on the top."

They climbed the slope to where the nine-pound

cannon was located. It was evening and the sun was disappearing over the horizon. They pretended to be stragglers sitting on the grass, enjoying the view.

"Are we sitting in the right spot?" asked Lina.

"Seems so," said Kuan Hee. "The cannon barrel is directly behind me and we are about five feet from the low wall."

"Let's start work," said Tim. "I'll keep an eye out for the soldiers."

They had come prepared with some short wooden sticks, which they were now using to dig the soil in front of them. Kuan Hee and Navin had their backs to the cannon, while Tim and Lina had the cannon in their sights.

Shortly, there was the clanking sound of metal. Kuan Hee and Navin pushed the soil aside and, lo and behold, a round metal plate a metre wide appeared in view. It had two handles on it. Kuan Hee tried to lift it. He couldn't. It was shut fast. Kuan Hee and Navin tried together in vain. Tim was the strongest of the three men. He and Navin heaved and pulled. They gasped and tried again. Years of exposure to the elements had adhered the hatch to the frame. It was a good fifteen minutes before the hatch gave way. It creaked open to the delight of the four friends. The sand around the edges of the hatch fell into the opening.

"Get out your LED flashlights," said Tim. "We are going in. I'll go first."

One after another, they jumped into the tunnel and hunched their way into the small room Mr Hon had described to them. Their LED flashlights lit up the place. It was slightly smaller than Mr Hon's living room. It was concrete everywhere, from the floor to the walls and the ceiling. There were water stains on the ceiling and the walls. Years of neglect had caused damp to build up in the room. The mushy stench of damp air was strong.

"Here, put some tissue paper over your nose," Kuan Hee told Lina.

"Don't close the hatch, or we'll suffocate here," said

Kuan Hee. "I forgot to ask Mr Hon whether there is ventilation in the tunnel."

"If we leave the hatch open, the soldiers might discover us," said Lina.

"Let's leave it open until we have opened the door in this room," said Tim.

"Who's going to try opening the door?" asked Kuan Hee.

"I will," said Tim. "I'm the strongest here. Let me do it."

There was a metal wheel on the wall in the room. It had emblems as Mr Hon had described. Tim followed the instructions Mr Hon had given and part of the wall rumbled open. There were steps going down.

"Let me go first," said Tim.

"Be careful," said Kuan Hee. He and Navin shone their flashlights into the darkness. It was a long tunnel.

"The air seems to be moving," said Tim. He was in the tunnel. "It's not that stale here."

"There must be air coming in from somewhere in the tunnel," said Navin as he and Kuan Hee joined Tim. "It's not that stuffy now." Lina went last. Kuan Hee stood by her side; unlike the three men who had been through national service, she was not used to such living conditions.

"I had better shut the hatch," said Tim. "Wait for me." He went back through the door. Meanwhile, Kuan Hee, Navin and Lina shone their flashlights at the ceiling, the walls and the floor. There were water stains everywhere. But surprisingly, there was no leak. The tunnel had been dug nearly a hundred years ago and it was testimony to the engineering skills of the British in the 1930s.

When Tim returned, the four friends walked along the tunnel. It was wide enough for them to walk abreast. The ceiling was about a metre taller than Tim, the tallest of the group. At regular intervals, there were oil lamps hanging on the walls. Navin grabbed one and peeped inside. There was no oil in it. He put it back on the wall hook. The tunnel meandered for about fifty metres and the four friends found themselves at the other end of the tunnel.

"It's the same type of wheel," said Tim. He pressed hard on the same two emblems and a creaking sound was heard as a door on the wall slid open about a metre from the floor.

"Shush," said Kuan Hee. Beyond the door was the drainage tunnel, and any loud noise they made could possibly echo in the bunker. They had to be careful lest they alerted the soldiers in the bunker.

"So far so good," said Navin. The others nodded in agreement.

"Let me go take a look," said Kuan Hee. "Don't worry, I will be careful." Lina had grabbed his shoulder tightly.

Kuan Hee lifted himself onto the floor of the drainage tunnel. He found himself in a long drain tunnel running perpendicular to the secret tunnel. On the floor, in the middle was a small drain. There was about a centimeter of water flowing in it. He could not stand; he couldn't even sit in the tunnel. There was only enough room for him to crawl through. Luckily, the manhole was less than two metres away. He elbowed his way towards the manhole, holding the flashlight in one hand. There was light filtering through the manhole cover into the drainage tunnel. *Must be from the light in the bunker*, Kuan Hee thought.

Kuan Hee stopped just below the manhole cover. He listened hard for sounds coming from above him. There was none. It was eerily quiet. *There's no one in the passageway*, he thought. *Should I or shouldn't I?*

Perspiration trickled down his forehead. The air was stale in the drainage tunnel. He placed both hands on the metal cover. It was cold. *The air-conditioning is switched on*, he told himself. He pressed against the cover. It moved. He lifted the cover slightly. The light from the bunker filtered through the edges of the cover. He peered through the small opening. There was no one in the passageway. Cool air breezed past his face. It was a welcome change from the humid drainage tunnel. *Must get back to the others,* Kuan Hee told himself. He let the metal cover slip back into position and made his way back to the tunnel.

"So how was it?" asked Tim. Kuan Hee flashed the OK sign with his hand and Tim shut the door.

"Let's talk outside," Kuan Hee said. The four friends walked back to the start of the tunnel and emerged from the hatch next to the nine-pound cannon.

At a McDonald's outlet in the nearby YMCA building, the four friends treated themselves to icy cold soft drinks. It was welcome nourishment after all the hard work they had put in this evening.

"So, are we good to go?" asked Navin in a low voice.

"I am happy to report—the manhole cover can be lifted with the slightest force," said Kuan Hee. "And the manhole opens into the passageway."

"That's what I call real good news," said Tim. The others nodded.

"So when do we strike?" asked Navin.

"Not yet," said Kuan Hee. "I still need to make contact with my mum and dad—confirm where they will be at dawn, and tell them our plan."

"Tell your parents not to leak the news of the rescue," said Tim. "We don't know whether the other researchers can be trusted. Remember—they were kidnapped. One of the researchers could be a spy."

"Tim's right, Kuan Hee," said Navin. "It has to be a surprise lightning operation."

"Yes, Kuan Hee," said Lina. "I agree with the others."

"OK," said Kuan Hee. "Lina and I will make the next trip here. You guys just wait for news. I'll book a room at the hotel across from the exit. Lina and I will spend a night at the hotel. We will observe the Battle Box's exterior for a whole day and night. We need to know the soldiers' movements."

"We can talk to your parents through little Busy," said Lina.

"That's the idea," said Kuan Hee.

"*Wah!* You two so lucky *ah*," said Navin, "having a romantic escapade without us."

"You are bad. Stop teasing us, Navin," said Lina.

CHAPTER 17

The Colonial Hotel stood halfway up the Fort Canning Hill, with its back facing the steep slope where the Battle Box's exit stood. It was originally the administration building of the British Far East Command Headquarters. From the windows of the hotel suite that Kuan Hee and Lina were spending the night in, they had an unhindered view of the bunker's exit. The entire walkway outside the bunker, stretching from the guardhouse on the left to the beginning of the reservoir on the right was within sight.

In the same way, these two hotel guests had no privacy as passers-by on the walkway had a clear view of the interior of the hotel room. But this was of the least importance to Kuan Hee and Lina who were spending the night there solely to watch the bunker. Only they had to be discreet in their activities so as not to arouse suspicion.

The pair took hourly turns to watch the slope and record the activities of the soldiers across from them. They saw soldiers bringing lunch and dinner and noted the times. They counted the number of soldiers on duty for each shift. They jotted down the times the soldiers made their rounds along the walkway. The glaring afternoon sun mellowed into a hazy orange ball before disappearing below the horizon and dark grey clouds swarmed across the skies, bringing evening.

Kuan Hee had left the television on. Channel five was now showing a local drama serial but the pair was not watching.

It was the Ngoh Shi Ping who got the attention of the pair. The former Transport Minister was on the air telling a news reporter he and twenty-three ex-Green Party MPs had joined the Unity Party. They would be contesting the by-elections this month. Next, the Unity Party's secretary-general Tan Eng Chai went on air to welcome the new members to his party. He said Ngoh Shi Ping would take the post of assistant-secretary-general in the party. He called for the public to support the party in the by-elections.

"This guy Ngoh Shi Ping did the right thing," said Kuan Hee. "I am glad he had the guts to stand up to Ong Chwee Seng."

"Will the Unity Party win the by-elections?" asked Lina.

"They will win seats all right. But they must win at least twenty of the parliamentary seats that are up for grabs," said Kuan Hee, "for the Green Party to lose their two-thirds majority in parliament. If it happens, it will be a good thing. At least, the Green Party can't carry on enacting laws at their whim and fancy, disregarding us ordinary folks."

"How many seats does the Green Party need to win to keep their two-third majority?" asked Lina.

"Let's see—four," said Kuan Hee.

"Only four?" said Lina. "Won't that be super easy?"

"Let's cross our fingers," said Kuan Hee, "and hope people will not vote for the Green Party."

"Are we attending the launching of the Unity Party's manifesto at Speakers' Corner tomorrow afternoon?" asked Lina.

"Yes," asked Kuan Hee. "It would be good to hear what the Unity Party has to say. I'll get the others to meet us there."

Soon it was time for Kuan Hee to launch little Busy into action. It was past midnight and the soldiers making their rounds along the walkway had disappeared from view. The pair had half an hour before the soldiers reappeared in front of the exit.

Kuan Hee unfolded the remote control and placed it on his lap. He and Lina sat on the floor in the balcony, leaning on pillows placed against the wall. Through the clear glass panels on the railings, they could see the slope in its entirety.

Little Busy flew out of Professor Wang's pocket, giving the pair a view of the room they were held in. It was about the size of a HDB kitchen. His parents shared the same room. They were asleep on two single beds placed at right angles to each other. Where the beds met was a rectangular table on which stood a table lamp and a clock. Against the opposite wall was a small desk and chair. There were apparently no other occupants.

Kuan Hee was reluctant to wake his parents; he was sure it was difficult for them to fall asleep in such a hostile environment, and if they were already in slumberland, he should not interrupt their sleep.

It was Lina who spoke through little Busy's speakers into Professor Wang's ear.

"Uncle, it's me, Lina," she said. "Uncle, wake up, please."

Professor Wang stirred. He scratched his shoulder and peered through half-opened eyelids. Then he reached for his glasses on the small table.

"Uncle, it's Lina," she said. "Kuan Hee's with me."

Professor Wang sat up and leaned towards little Busy.

"Kuan Hee's with you?" he said in a low voice.

"Dad," said Kuan Hee. "How are you? How's Mum?"

Professor Wang shook his wife. "Dear, Kuan Hee's here," he said. "Wake up, dear."

Mrs Wang turned. Then she sat up and looked at little Busy. She smiled into the little robot housefly's eyes. "Kuan Hee, It's you," she whispered.

"Mum and Dad, I missed you guys," said Kuan Hee.

"So did we, Kuan Hee," said Professor Wang. "Where are you? Are you nearby?"

"We are opposite, in The Colonial Hotel," said Kuan Hee. "We have been here the whole night watching the bunker."

"Uncle and Auntie, did they treat you well?" asked Lina.

"They have been nice to us," said Mrs Wang, "but I don't like it here. This place gives me the creeps."

"Dad, we are going to get you and Mum out," said Kuan Hee. "Listen carefully. The day after tomorrow, just before dawn, we'll come for you."

"What about my staff, Kuan Hee?" said Professor Wang. "I can't leave them here."

"We'll take them with us too," said Kuan Hee. "But, Dad, please don't tell them about the rescue. One of them could be a spy. He could spoil our plan."

"I understand, Kuan Hee," said Professor Wang.

"Dad, are you locked in your room?" asked Kuan Hee.

"They lock us up every night," said Professor Wang. "Then they leave the bunker. But they come in to check on us now and then."

"What sort of lock do they use for the door?" asked Kuan Hee.

"Padlock," said Professor Wang. "Steel padlock."

"Thanks, Dad," said Kuan Hee.

"It's the day after tomorrow—Friday, right?" said Professor Wang.

"Yes, Dad—5:00 a.m. on Friday," said Kuan Hee.

"There are many guards here," said Professor Wang. "And they are armed with rifles."

"Don't worry, Dad," said Kuan Hee. "We aren't going to charge out of the bunker with you. We are taking a secret route below the bunker. It goes all the way to the nine-pound cannon."

"A secret tunnel under the bunker?" said Professor Wang in astonishment.

"Yes," said Kuan Hee. "Tim and Navin are helping me. So is Lina's elder brother. We'll get you and Mum out for sure."

"Kuan Hee, how did you know we are here?" asked Professor Wang.

"Brigadier Walmsley told me," said Kuan Hee. "He's the one who found you. He said he couldn't use the Special Forces to rescue you and the others, but he will back us up on the day of the rescue."

"So the Brigadier has found us finally," said Professor Wang. "Kuan Hee, there's something you must know."

The shuffle of feet echoed in the silence of the night. Someone was approaching the room. The pair was so engrossed in conversation with Kuan Hee's parents that they had forgotten to keep a watch on the bunker's exit.

"Quick, leave, Kuan Hee" said Professor Wang. "They are here to check on us."

"Remember Mum and Dad, 5:00 a.m. Friday," said Kuan Hee.

Little Busy flitted into the professor's palm. He clasped it and placed it in his pocket.

"Kuan Hee, now that your parents are taken care of, let's not waste time," said Lina. "Shall we?"

"Here, on the floor?" said Kuan Hee.

"No *lah*, silly," said Lina. "The big bed's been waiting for us since this afternoon."

"People can see us from the slope," said Kuan Hee.

"Who cares," said Lina. She turned off the lights in the room.

CHAPTER 18

It was the second time that Kuan Hee and Lina were meeting Brigadier Walmsley at ToastBox Café in Plaza Singapura. This time, the Brigadier was waiting for them in the alfresco section of the café. He was the perfect picture of a tourist as he sat wearing his hunting hat and flipping through a tourist guide.

The Brigadier, ever the gentleman, stood up as Lina took her seat opposite him. Kuan Hee ordered beverages for himself and Lina as Brigadier Walmsley had a *kopi oh kosong* in front of him. He returned with the drinks and sat next to Lina.

"You know, I never can get used to the heat here," said the Brigadier. He wiped the sweat off his forehead and behind his ears.

"Mr Walmsley, we can sit in the air-conditioned section of the café," said Lina.

"But I like the sun," said the Brigadier. "I like getting a tan." The pair smiled. They were used to the Brigadier's whimsical mannerisms.

The Brigadier patted the back of his hair as he sat in thought. The two ladies at the next table vacated their seats and a café assistant came to clear the table. Seeing there was no one within earshot, the Brigadier launched into conversation.

"What news do you have for me, Kuan Hee?" the Brigadier asked.

"My parents and the other researchers are indeed at the bunker," said Kuan Hee. "They are safe and sound."

"That's good news," said the Brigadier. "How many researchers?"

"Six," said Kuan Hee, "not counting my mum and dad."

"That's correct," said the Brigadier. "All research staff accounted for. Kuan Hee, what are your plans?"

"Friday 5:00 a.m., that's when we strike," said Kuan Hee. "We'll use a secret tunnel below the bunker." He unfolded a map of the bunker Mr Hon had given him and set it on the small table.

"My parents and the researchers are in these three rooms," said Kuan Hee, pointing them out on the map. "The secret tunnel runs from this manhole to the nine-pound cannon over here." He moved his fingers across the map to the cannon symbol.

"I see," said the Brigadier. "So you avoid the guards altogether. Smart move."

"Mr Walmsley, can you arrange for transport to wait here?" asked Kuan Hee. His finger was now resting on Canning Rise, next to the Gothic Gate.

"May I?" said Mr Walmsley. He took out his smartphone and activated the camera. Kuan Hee nodded and the Brigadier snapped pictures of the map.

"Kuan Hee, I will take care of the transport," said the Brigadier. "My people will take over at the Gothic Gate. They will move your parents and the researchers to a safe place. Do you need firepower?"

"We hope to pull off the whole thing without firing a single shot," said Kuan Hee in an almost inaudible voice. "But we are prepared. We have three SAR21s and a Steyr SSG 69."

"Gosh, how did you get your hands on them?" asked the Brigadier.

"Long story, Mr Walmsley," said Kuan Hee.

"You guys sure are capable. I must take my hat off to you," said the Brigadier. "By the way, do you have a back-up plan?"

"Back-up plan?" said Kuan Hee. He was caught off-balance. He had not thought of a back-up plan.

"Every operation must have a contingency plan," said the Brigadier as Kuan Hee looked uneasily at the Brigadier.

"We forgot," said Lina, racing to Kuan Hee's rescue.

"It's alright," said the Brigadier. "Kuan Hee, keep the communication channel on Google Glass open. Update me as the rescue progresses. If something goes wrong, my people will take over. We will be the back-up plan. You just get your parents and the researchers to safety. And if you hear any noises outside, ignore them. It's my people in action."

"Yes, Mr Walmsley," said Kuan Hee. He had recovered the use of his tongue. "I am sorry I left out a back-up plan."

"No worries," said the Brigadier. "Happens to the best of us. So in a nutshell, I'll take over if something goes wrong. OK?"

"OK," said the pair in unison.

"Godspeed," said the Brigadier.

CHAPTER 19

It was a packed day for Kuan Hee and Lina. No sooner had they checked out of The Colonial Hotel than they met the Brigadier at ToastBox Café in Plaza Singapura. Now, they were on their way to attend the Unity Party's manifesto launch in Hong Lim Park.

Speakers' Corner was a flat open field, almost the size of two football fields. Behind a long concrete platform, across the road were glass-clad high-rise buildings. On the opposite side was a smattering of pre-war shophouses, alongside which was a two-storey colonial-era building now housing a police post.

This evening, the field was flooded with people—office workers from the nearby office buildings and others from across the island. The young and the old—they were all here to listen to what the Unity Party had to offer in the upcoming by-elections. It was a mass of bobbing heads as far as the eye could see. In the warm glow of light globes placed around the perimeter of the field, the spectators stood, eyeing the platform where the Unity Party's leaders sat.

The four friends mingled with the other spectators barely two metres from the platform steps, where party minders kept a wary eye on the crowd. Patches of dark blue marked the positions of policemen in the crowd.

It was a subdued mood that greeted the first speaker on the platform. Tan Eng Chai, the Unity Party's secretary general poured scorn on the Green Party government for restricting people's freedom and creating an atmosphere of fear in Singapore.

Next, Ngoh Shi Ping's voice blared over the loud speakers. He called on the government to arbitrarily release the protesters it had detained and stop the unlawful use of computer judges in the courts to try the detainees. He also condemned the government's house raids on opposition party members.

"I actually came here to hear what Ngoh Shi Ping will do to rein in Ong Chwee Seng if he is elected," said Kuan Hee. "So far, besides complaining, he hasn't done anything else."

"Let's not be impatient, Kuan Hee," said Navin. "The night is young."

"Shush, he's talking about Ong Chwee Seng now," said Lina.

"He's saying Ong Chwee Seng is a two-faced liar," said Tim.

"It's clear to one and all this chap Ong Chwee Seng is a phony," said Kuan Hee.

"He's calling a spade a spade," said Navin.

"He's being frank. Will he get into trouble?" said Lina.

"I hear he and Ong Chwee Seng were schoolmates," said Tim. "Ong Chwee Seng was the one who got him into politics."

"Now they are standing on opposite sides of the fence," said Lina. "Do you think Ong Chwee Seng will turn on his schoolmate?"

"No prizes for guessing," said Kuan Hee.

Suddenly, there was a loud explosion. Plumes of smoke fanned out across the field, blanketing the spectators in the middle of the field. There were cries of pain and panic as shrapnel from the explosion flew. Several spectators were injured. In the ensuing pandemonium, some spectators were trampled over.

Fortunately, the four friends were spared injury; they were standing near the platform. Just then, a score of soldiers filed past them. Some formed a cordon around the platform while others climbed the platform and grabbed hold of Ngoh Shi Ping, Tan Eng Chai and their comrades. The Unity Party's minders could only watch helplessly as the soldiers had brandished their rifles. The soldiers whisked them away in a bus.

"Gosh! The Unity Party leaders have been detained," said Navin. "It's a violation of human rights. This is a peaceful assembly."

"You think the soldiers care a damn?" said Tim.

"Being schoolmates also no use," said Lina.

"It's the politics of power," said Kuan Hee. "Some famous fellow once said: Power tends to corrupt, and absolute power corrupts absolutely."

"What about the by-elections?" Lina asked. "Will the Unity Party leaders be able to participate in the by-elections?"

CHAPTER 20

The sun was descending beyond the blocks of HDB flats in the distance when Kuan Hee and Lina got out of bed. The evening brought a hazy glow that lasted past sunset. It was that time of the year when the burning of forests and peatland in Indonesia ushered in hazy skies across the island. But it was no cause for complaint for the pair this time, for hazy conditions made for better cover when they were mounting their rescue of Kuan Hee's parents and the researchers at the Battle Box.

After dinner, Kuan Hee, Lina, Navin and Tim huddled on the floor of the small room above the shophouse in Realty Park. The smell of lubricating oil punctuated the air. Tim and Navin were cleaning the SAR21s they had retrieved from a hiding place. Kuan Hee was dismantling a Steyr SSG 69 and wiping its parts. He dragged a small rag through its barrel several times and peered inside. Tim and Navin had done a good job oiling the weapons before stashing them away.

"I don't see the cutting tool," said Tim. "Have you forgotten it?"

"My brother will bring it later," said Lina.

"I forgot—he's coming with us too," said Tim.

"He won't go into the bunker with us," said Kuan Hee. "He'll wait in the van on Canning Rise."

"The Brigadier's men will be on Canning Rise too?" asked Navin.

"Yes, they will take my parents and the researchers to a safe place," said Kuan Hee. "And, in case the plan fails, his men will take over."

"It won't fail, will it?" said Lina.

"Of course not," said Kuan Hee. But his voice lacked the brashness it usually displayed.

"Can I go into the tunnel with you?" asked Lina.

"I thought the matter is settled," said Tim. "that you are to stay on the grass slope next to the hatch."

"She insists on tagging along," said Kuan Hee.

"But she can't come with us," said Navin, "It's too dangerous. Besides, she will hinder our work."

"Yeah, I agree with Navin," said Tim. "We can't be looking out for her in the tunnel."

"It's decided then," said Kuan Hee. "You stay on the grass slope."

Lina could not hide her disappointment. But she didn't cry as she usually would. She knew the safety of Kuan Hee's parents depended on the success of tonight's rescue operation. She held back her tears.

"So Lina watches the hatch. Navin stays in the end of the tunnel next to the drainage system. Tim and I will enter the bunker," said Kuan Hee. "Tim will cover me. I will cut the padlocks."

"You sure the cutters can do the job?" said Navin.

"It can cut through steel and titanium," said Kuan Hee. "It cut through the wrist tag the army put on my wrist. Anyway, we've got Alex the robot."

"Gosh, I forgot about the robots," said Tim. "Are you taking both robots along?"

"Yes, of course. But we will only use Alex's laser weapon system if there's no choice," said Kuan Hee. "It's very powerful. It may destroy the entire door."

"Have we forgotten anything?" asked Lina.

"Let's see. Weapons, ammunition, earphones, LED flashlights," said Tim.

"We've got them all," said Kuan Hee.

"Don't forget our Google Glass devices," said Lina.

"What time do we move?" asked Navin.

"My brother says there are roadblocks around the island after midnight," said Lina. "He says it is safer if we travel before midnight. He'll be here at 11:15 p.m."

"That's about an hour from now," said Navin. He fished a pack of cigarettes from his pocket, took out one and lit it. He took a long puff on it. Tim sensed his uneasiness. "We'll be fine. Trust me."

The trees were swaying in the open field across the shophouses as the four friends walked along the five-foot-way towards the van. Some trees were bowing more than the others as the wind swept across the open space. It was too dark to see if the grey clouds were rain clouds. The red tint in the skies gave a hint of the weather to come.

The team squeezed into the rear of Lina's brother's van, next to two large tool boxes which were a fixture in the van. Their weapons and ammo were hidden in their backpacks. Lina's brother sat with his son, Xaden, in front of the van.

"Xaden wanted to come along to help," said Lina's brother. "He will stay in the van with me."

"I am in the National Cadet Corps," said Xaden. "So I know a little about rescue work."

"More hands, less work," said Kuan Hee.

"The more, the merrier," said Tim.

A pair of cutters hung alongside several umbrellas on the metal rack between the driver's section and the rear. Tim took it and placed it in his backpack. It was so long that its handles peeped out of the backpack.

"The wind is too strong for my liking," said Navin. "Maybe, rain is coming."

"Hope not," said Kuan Hee.

The van cruised through the suburban housing estates and arrived at the outskirts of the city where the bright city lights accentuated the redness of the skies.

"Look! The window is misting," said Lina. "It must be too cold in here."

"It's not mist," Kuan Hee said. "It's raindrops." Alas, the rain was here. Within seconds, heavy rain pelted on the windows of the van. The occupants of the van could no longer see the outside.

"So how about the mission?" asked Navin.

"Full steam ahead," said Tim.

"I agree," said Kuan Hee. "There's no turning back." It was too late to postpone the rescue operation, for his parents and the researchers were waiting anxiously in the bunker.

"Lina, you remain in the van," said Kuan Hee.

"But, I want to go with you," said Lina.

"You can't be standing in the rain," said Kuan Hee. "For goodness's sake, we don't know how long it will take us in the bunker."

Lina tilted her head. Her eyes stared upwards at Kuan Hee and her lips tightened into a scrowl. Kuan Hee knew he had to make a concession or the mission could be in jeopardy.

Tim came to the rescue. "Lina, you can hide from the rain in the tunnel," he said. Lina's face lightened up at once. On her, little things worked wonders.

It was pouring cats and dogs when the van came to a stop along Canning Rise. Kuan Hee looked at his watch. The time was 11:55 p.m.

"The good thing about this heavy rain," said Navin, "is nobody comes out for patrol duty."

"Yeah, it's a godsend," said Tim, trying to make light of an unexpected situation.

"Keep your smartphones on," reminded Lina's brother. The team members launched the Zello app on their phone screens. The app provided them with a private channel for communicating with one another.

"Keep your earphones in your ears at all times," said Kuan Hee. "And provide updates to the others in the network." They used rubber bands to fasten the earphones over their ears. It was uncomfortable but necessary. It was simply not practical for them to be holding their smartphones all the time.

Kuan Hee commanded Alex and Xander to come out of the backpacks. The robots climbed onto his lap.

"Kuan Hee, activate your Google Glass," said Lina. "You have to update Brigadier Walmsley during the mission."

"Ten-four," said Kuan Hee.

The team jumped out into the rain, along with Alex and Xander. They were only halfway up the steps along the slope but they were wet to their skin. It was a torrential downpour that had fallen tonight. The rapidly flowing water on the steps made their climb more difficult. Lina slipped and almost fell but for Kuan Hee who was holding on to her arms. It was impossible to see the cannon. Visibility was down to a few metres ahead of them. Tim found the spot where the hatch was. He groped around in the soil for the handles. He found them and, with Kuan Hee, managed to lift the hatch. The rain poured into the hole.

"Be careful, it's slippery down there," said Tim. "I'll go down first."

One by one they entered the hole in the ground. Navin, who was last in, closed the hatch above him. There were puddles of water on the floor in the room below the cannon. But no more water was coming through the hatch opening now. Although they were drenched, they didn't feel cold; it was warm in the room.

Tim walked to the metal wheel on the wall, pressed two emblems on its spokes, and the door on the wall creaked open. The team moved down the steps into the long tunnel.

"Ready your weapons," said Tim. "This is no walk in the park, you know." The three men took out their SAR21s, snapped the magazines into place, and grasped the pistol grips. The SSG 69 was in Lina's backpack.

Kuan Hee ordered Alex and Xander to move ahead in the tunnel. The two robots took long strides to keep ahead of the team, for they were merely thirty-centimetres tall. Speaking with Brigadier Walmsley on Google Glass's communication app, Kuan Hee learnt the Brigadier's men were on site.

At the end of the tunnel, the team sat down together, resting their rifles against the wall. They were about five hours early. It was to be a long wait in the stuffy tunnel. They looked at one another in askance. Kuan Hee took out little Busy's remote and activated the robot housefly. It wriggled out of Professor Wang's pocket. Both his parents were awake. They were sitting on the bed next to each other.

"Kuan Hee, you are here," said Professor Wang. "Your mum and I couldn't sleep. We thought we should wait."

"We are in the tunnel behind the drainage system, Dad," said Kuan Hee. "Lina, Tim, and Navin are with me."

"I told my staff about the rescue at dinner time," said Professor Wang. "They are all excited."

"Have the guards come in to check on you?" asked Kuan Hee.

"Yes, about fifteen minutes ago," said Professor Wang. "Their next round is at 3:00 a.m."

"Kuan Hee, can we move up the rescue operation?" asked Tim. "Now is a good time. It's pouring outside. Nobody in his right mind will come in through the rain."

"Yeah, I agree with Tim," said Navin. "The five-hour wait is too long."

"Let me check with the Brigadier first," said Kuan Hee. He removed his earphones and spoke into the Google

Glass's microphone. Then he turned to his team.

"The Brigadier agrees. We move at 12:30 a.m. His men are in black and wearing balaclava," said Kuan Hee.

He spoke through little Busy's speaker to tell his parents the rescue would be brought forward.

The team spent the next few minutes in nervous concentration. Their hands were clammy on the pistol grips, but it wasn't because of the damp air in the tunnel.

Kuan Hee climbed into the drainage tunnel after Tim had opened the door. With his SAR21 alongside him, he crawled a few metres to the manhole. Alex walked ahead. There was no need for it to bend; the tunnel was twice its height. Tim was next into the tunnel. It was a squeeze for him as he had his backpack on.

Hearing no sound above him, Kuan Hee lifted the manhole cover slightly. The bunker's lights penetrated the drainage tunnel, and Alex's metallic silver body glistened. He looked back at Tim to signal he was going to enter the bunker. He pushed aside the metal cover and let Alex climb on top of him. He lifted himself onto the floor of the bunker and readied his SAR21. Tim climbed onto the floor and knelt in the opposite direction.

"All clear," said Tim. "No cameras."

Alex stayed at Kuan Hee's heels as the two men tiptoed through the passageway towards the room where Kuan Hee's parents were held. It was the first room on the right at the fork in the passageway. The next two rooms were where the researchers were sleeping. The fourth room was where they had seen the guards' rifle rack.

While Tim kept a watch at the fork in the passageway, Kuan Hee sidled up to the guards' room. The door was open. He looked inside. The room was empty. He gave a thumbs-up signal to Tim and Tim came up behind him.

"The soldiers are not in; they must be in the guardhouse," said Kuan Hee.

"I'll watch the exit," said Tim. He passed the pair of long cutters to Kuan Hee.

Kuan Hee instructed Alex to watch the passageway; the robot had heat-sensing capability in his glassy eyes. It could detect anyone coming its way and raise the alarm.

The cutters sliced through the shackles of the padlock effortlessly. Pieces of the padlock fell with a thud. The sound reverberated through the passageway. Kuan Hee hesitated and then opened the metal door. His parents were behind the door. They hugged him; his mother planted kisses on his face. Professor Wang pulled her away.

"Time is precious," Professor Wang told his wife. "These little things can wait."

The couple huddled outside the door while Kuan Hee went over to the next two rooms. Within seconds, he had the doors opened. The six researchers, wearing the look of relief, joined his parents in the passageway. With Kuan Hee leading the way and Tim at the tail of the group, everyone made for the manhole.

Kuan Hee leapt into the drainage tunnel, followed by his mum, dad and the researchers. One by one they crawled to the tunnel doorway. Tim made sure the group had cleared the doorway before jumping into the manhole with Alex. He replaced the metal cover. Perspiration was dripping down his face onto his neck and his hands were wet from sweat. *So far so good,* he told himself.

Lina squealed in delight on seeing Kuan Hee's parents. She went up to his mother and hugged her excitedly. Navin waved his hand to say hello to them.

"No time to lose," said Kuan Hee. "Come, let's go."

With an uneasy gait, the motley group moved to the other end of the tunnel, into the room below the cannon.

Kuan Hee and Navin stepped into the tunnel next to the room. They raised their rifles and pointed them at the hatch. Tim moved past them He placed his hands on the hatch handles. They all paused.

One. Two. Three.

Then the hatch creaked open. Rainwater poured into

the tunnel. The rain pelted Tim. *Good, the coast is clear,* Tim told himself. He lifted himself onto the grassy slope and grabbed the SAR21 Navin had handed him. He knelt next to the opening and held the rifle close to his face, with his hand on the pistol grip. Navin was next to poke his head out of the opening in the ground. He took up position next to Tim. He watched the opposite direction. Then Kuan Hee's parents, the researchers and Lina climbed onto the muddy grass. They wiped their faces. The rain had drenched them. Kuan Hee was the last to come out of the tunnel. Alex was by his side.

Then, without warning, shots rang out in the distance. Some soldiers had appeared on top of the slope, behind the fence. They were shooting at the group.

"Quick! Make a run for it," Tim screamed as he opened fire at the top of the slope. He could hardly see the fence; he was shooting blindly. Navin led Kuan Hee's parents and the researchers down the steps towards the Gothic Gate. Lina refused to move. She wanted to be with Kuan Hee, who by now had climbed onto the grassy slope with Alex. The hail of bullets continued. The pair was in the line of fire. They staggered down the slope, with Kuan Hee pushing Lina in front of him.

There was more gunfire. This time, the shots came from the direction of the Registry of Marriages. They came from high-powered rifles. Some of the soldiers on top of the slope fell. But more soldiers appeared along the perimeter fencing. The whole platoon had congregated at the cannon. Some soldiers had climbed over the fence and were about to jump onto the grassy slope. More shots rang out. One by one, the soldiers fell onto the ground; their lifeless bodies lay sprawled on the grass.

Two vans screeched to a stop along Canning Rise. The doors opened and balaclava-clad men jumped out. They bundled Professor Wang, his wife and the researchers into the backs of the vans. Lina's brother's van was nowhere in sight. Two hooded men, MP5 sub-machine guns slung over their chests, towered over Tim and Navin in front of the vans. They were waiting for Kuan Hee and Lina.

Lina and Kuan Hee reached the vans. Lina's face was a picture of desperation. She was clinging on to Kuan Hee, and crying. Kuan Hee was clutching his chest. He fell in front of the men. There was blood on the back of his shirt; he had been shot. One of the hooded men dashed towards the slope to retrieve Kuan Hee's rifle, while another helped Kuan Hee into the first van. His parents were in it. His mother was hysterical; his father was the picture of calm as he pressed gauze pads onto Kuan Hee's back.

With Tim and Navin on board too, the first van rolled down Canning Rise onto the main road. The second van followed. Behind them, the reports of gunfire continued. The Brigadier's men were still at work on the slope, trying to delay the soldiers' advance.

"Alex. Alex," groaned Kuan Hee. He was delirious.

"Alex is here," said Professor Wang. "It is safe." But Kuan Hee continued mumbling.

The vans raced through Dhoby Ghaut into Selegie Road. Then, at the junction of Selegie and Rochor Roads, they parted ways. The first van, with the team and Kuan Hee's parents cruised into Bukit Timah Road, while the second moved into Serangoon Road. Apparently, they were heading to different destinations.

The first van stopped along the side of the road and a man in the front of the van came over to open the side door. He was no longer wearing a balaclava. The commando was a Caucasian with a tanned face and neck almost the width of a tree trunk. He was holding a longish device in his hand. He waved the device over the occupants of the van and shook his head at the driver, another Caucasian. Once he was back in the passenger seat, the van resumed its journey to an unknown destination.

CHAPTER 21

A popular bible verse goes:

> To every thing there is a season,
> and a time to every purpose under the heaven:
> A time to be born, and a time to die;

In his exploits with his *kakis*, Kuan Hee had had the misfortune to be shot three times. The first time, five years ago, left him with a shoulder wound. The second time, not long ago, saw him injured in the shoulder again. The third time was today. He had been twice lucky the last two times. Would he be able to escape death again? Or was today for him a time to die?

Not if Lina could help it. Not if Brigadier Walmsley had the best that America's special forces could offer.

Kuan Hee, Lina, and his parents were whisked away by speedboat to a ship anchored south of Singapore, near the Indonesian islands of Batam-Rempang-Galang.

From afar, the ship had the outlines of a cargo ship. The US Navy had a fleet of these quasi-civilian ships operating around the world. It had a nondescript name—maritime support vessel—that betrayed its capabilities.

With a displacement of 40,000 tons, the ship could hold two hundred and fifty men easily. It provided the navy with the ability to strike within eight hundred nautical miles of the ship. A helicopter landing pad; a hangar big enough to house Apache attack helicopters and Little Birds; and a rear ramp for vehicles amply qualifed the ship for special operations work.

The ship also had a specially fitted operating theatre and a team of medical personnel. It was this team who attended to Kuan Hee on board the ship.

Kuan Hee woke up on the seventh day of their stay on the ship.

"Where am I?" asked Kuan Hee.

"We are on board the Artemis," said Lina.

"Thank heavens you are alright," said Mrs Wang.

"We are on a ship?" said Kuan Hee.

"Yes, dear. You have been unconscious for a week," said Mrs Wang. She fondled Kuan Hee's hair and stroked his face. "I'm glad you have pulled through."

"Where's Dad? Is he OK?" asked Kuan Hee.

"Your father is with Brigadier Walmsley," said Mrs Wang. "We have been worried sick about you. Lina hasn't slept a wink since you were shot."

Kuan Hee looked at Lina. Indeed, pimples had broken out on her cheeks. There were black rings around her eyes. She had not been sleeping well. But for these, she was a picture of health. Kuan Hee was glad she was unhurt. He had taken a bullet meant for her, but it was his duty to protect her. After all, she was his world.

Kuan Hee tried to sit up. He grimaced. *It must be a pretty bad hit that I took this time,* he told himself. His mother raised the head of the bed so he could look out of the porthole.

"We are in the middle of the ocean," said Kuan Hee.

"No *lah*, we are off Batam," said Lina. "About forty-five minutes away from Singapore."

"Yes, dear. Lina's right. We are on an American

military vessel," said Mrs Wang.

"You are pretty lucky," said a voice from behind his mother.

The Brigadier had entered the room with Professor Wang. He was not wearing his hunting hat. He stood next to Kuan Hee and Lina.

"Three times lucky," said the Brigadier. "You better hope there's no fourth time."

"*Choy!*" said Lina. She glared at the Brigadier. "Mr Walmsley, how can you curse him?"

"Lina, the Brigadier was just jesting," said Professor Wang. "Don't be so serious."

"My apologies, Lina," said the Brigadier. "Don't take this to heart."

"Mr Walmsley, thanks a million," said Kuan Hee. "I couldn't have made it without your help."

"It's the other way round, Kuan Hee," said the Brigadier. "The US government should be thanking you and your friends for helping to rescue the researchers. Well done."

Lina was beaming. *My Kuan Hee is a hero in others' eyes,* she told herself.

"When will I be able to get off this bed?" asked Kuan Hee.

"The doctor says you need a few more days of complete rest," said Mrs Wang.

"Yes, don't stress your body," said the Brigadier. "Don't just think of yourself. Look after your body well too."

"Your mother and I are heading to Fort Bragg in North Carolina," said Professor Wang.

"Is it going to be really safe this time?" Kuan Hee asked himself. His father was a magnet for trouble everywhere he went. *The base in Australia was supposed to be safe,* Kuan Hee thought. *Look what happened there. And the US government was none the wiser for a whole year.*

"Fort Bragg is the headquarters of the US Special

Forces," said the Brigadier. "There's no place safer than that." At once, goose pimples attacked Kuan Hee's arms. It was as if the Brigadier could read his mind.

"Dear, I think you and Lina should come with us," said Mrs Wang.

"Mum, I can't leave Singapore," Kuan Hee protested. "I've lived there all my life. I know of no other place."

"Me too, Auntie," said Lina. "I want to be with Kuan Hee wherever he goes."

"Kuan Hee, there's no place for you on the island," said Mrs Wang.

"Dear, let him do what he wants," said Professor Wang.

"But he's a wanted man there," said Mrs Wang. "If they catch him, there's no telling what they will do to him."

"I'll take good care of myself," said Kuan Hee. He held up his hand slightly and raised his index and middle fingers. "Promise, I will."

"We'll talk about this another day," said Professor Wang. "Let him rest, dear." He did not want the conversation to descend into an argument. The Professor knew his son would not waver once he had his heart set on doing something. Besides, he was doing good things for his country. *Why should I stop him from ridding the country of a tyrant?* Professor Wang thought. *Gosh! I have yet to tell him about the tyrant.*

The Brigadier and Kuan Hee's parents left the room, leaving the pair to themselves. Kuan Hee had many questions for Lina. He had been unconscious for several days and was curious about what had happened after the rescue.

"Where are Tim and Navin? Are they alright?"

"You are the only one injured. I think they should be home now. They were at the jetty to see us off."

"And the researchers?"

"They are on this ship too, except for one. The

Brigadier said he was the one who tipped off the soldiers. He activated a GPS tracker when we were in the bunker."

"The devil! He did? Which one is he?"

"The Brigadier didn't say and I didn't ask him."

"Did your brother get away alright?"

"The Brigadier's commandoes got to my brother before we arrived at the Gothic Gate. They told my brother to leave the place. Said they would take care of the transport."

"I didn't notice they weren't at the gate. Everything was moving so fast, and we were dodging bullets."

"You mean—getting in the bullets' way."

"Oh yeah. I guess you are right. Are AleXander with my dad?"

"No, they are under your bed, in your backpack."

"Is that so?" Kuan Hee leaned over the bed, trying to see under it.

"Be careful. You haven't fully recovered." Lina reached for the backpack and handed it to Kuan Hee. He opened it and gently handled Alex. He was looking for signs of damage.

"Don't be silly, Kuan Hee. He's almost indestructible. You said it yourself. He's made of a special titanium and gold alloy."

"Just making sure. Just making sure."

CHAPTER 22

A week later, Kuan Hee was able to move around on his own. The Brigadier showed him around the ship. Kuan Hee felt honoured, for it was supposed to be a secret military vessel. The two of them were now leaning against the railing on the deck of the ship. It was breezy and their hair was in a disheveled mess.

"Was this the ship my dad was taken to five years ago?" Kuan Hee asked.

"Yes, of course. Like you, he was operated on here. This ship is sort of a HQ for our special forces in the region. From it, we stage many missions—for the sake of regional security," said the Brigadier. "You know, Kuan Hee, the United States does not want to be an international policeman. But we have no choice. Tumoil in any part of the world puts democracy at risk. The United States is commited to protecting this fragile thing called democracy, even if people label us *kapoh*." *The Brigadier knows how to use 'kapoh', Kuan Hee thought. He certainly knows quite a few Singlish words.*

"I thought you said you couldn't use your commandoes in the rescue of my mum and dad?" said Kuan Hee.

"That was before the Singapore army's crackdown on

the opposition," said the Brigadier."They went past the tipping point. We had to act. Which is also why we are having this conversation today, Kuan Hee." *The Brigadier wants me to do something,* Kuan Hee told himself.

"The future lies in our hands, Kuan Hee," said the Brigadier. "You and I can change the future, if we want to."

"Yes, Mr Walmsley," said Kuan Hee. He wasn't sure what the Brigadier was getting at. The Brigadier had always been direct—till today.

"I had been wondering how I should put it," said the Brigadier. "Let me quote the words of a famous philosopher." He took a piece of paper from his pocket and unfolded it in front of Kuan Hee. On it, the Brigadier had written:

> There is no crueler tyranny than that which is perpetuated under the shield of law and in the name of justice.

"Charles de Montesquieu was a French philosopher," said the Brigadier. "I could be wrong, but I think he is the one who gave us the dictionary word 'despot'. The Green Party government is now only a shell of itself. Ong Chwee Seng is the Green Party government and vice versa. Do you copy?"

"You mean he is the one calling the shots?" said Kuan Hee.

"Yes, exactly. He is running the show at his whim and fancy. There is no one stopping him," said the Brigadier.

"You want me to stop him?" said Kuan Hee, with an incredulous gasp.

"Nope, not you—alone, that is," said the Brigadier, "but with other like-minded people. You strike me as someone who will stand up to injustice—correct wrongdoings. I saw this quality in you five years ago, when you led your peers in standing up to the military regime then. You were shot a few times doing it. You attacked an armored personnel carrier to save a fellow protester. In my mind, you have what it takes. Your country needs young people like you to lead it into the future."

"What do you want me to do, Mr Walmsley?" asked Kuan Hee.

"It's not what I want you to do, Kuan Hee," said the Brigadier, "rather what you can do for your country. The United States can give you a leg up. That's all we can do. The rest is up to young people like you—to put things right. Save the country from tyranny."

"I understand, Mr Walmsley," said Kuan Hee. "But, I am only one person. I can't do much."

"Of course, not you alone, Kuan Hee, but together with others," said the Brigadier. "You were once a student leader. I'm sure you can get in touch with many other young people. Get them to do national service. Get them to do something for their country—before it's too late."

"Here, take this note," said the Brigadier. "Reflect on the contents. I'm sure you will understand what it is saying."

Professor Wang appeared on the deck. He was looking for Kuan Hee.

"Ah, your father is here," said the Brigadier. "I'll take my leave. We'll continue this conversation later." The Brigadier left father and son on the deck.

Professor Wang had wanted to get something off his chest. He thought now was as good a time as any to tell Kuan Hee what he needed to know.

"Our arch enemy is alive," said Professor Wang to an unsuspecting Kuan Hee.

"Arch enemy?" said Kuan Hee. "What are you talking about, Dad?"

"Colonel Tee—the scourge of our lives—he is alive and well," said Professor Wang.

"But I thought Jordan killed him five years ago?" said Kuan Hee. "How can it be?"

"Son, I thought so, too," said Professor Wang. "He actually died, but his memories lived on then."

Kuan Hee was having difficulty understanding what his father was saying. He gave his father a blank look.

"Son, Colonel Tee had the master copy of his memories hidden somewhere. His henchmen wanted him back alive, so they kidnapped your mother and me. They forced me to do a memory transfer into another person."

"You mean, the same way you transferred his memories into Jordan?" said Kuan Hee.

"Exactly, son," said Professor Wang. "That's how he came alive again. And he is reprising his evil in the country. Nobody seems to be able to stop him. He is too powerful. I should have destroyed the master tapes when I had the chance. Now, the memory bank is in his hands."

"Dad, so his henchmen got soldiers to kidnap you in Australia and fly you back to Singapore?"

"Yes, son. He has got control of the army—in fact the entire country," said Professor Wang. "You should be able to guess whose body he has taken over."

"There is only one person who's all powerful now—the PM, Ong Chwee Seng?" said Kuan Hee.

"Yes, son. Colonel Tee is Ong Chwee Seng and Ong Chwee Seng is Colonel Tee," said Professor Wang.

"No wonder, this chap Ong Chwee Seng is no longer the person he was before he became PM," said Kuan Hee.

"Colonel Tee's men kidnapped him over a year ago. I did the operation about that time," said Professor Wang.

"So that's why Ong Chwee Seng is doing the same things Colonel Tee did to Singapore five years ago. The country is now totally under his control, Dad," said Kuan Hee.

"I am afraid so, son," said Professor Wang. "And this is only the start. There is no telling what Colonel Tee and his men will do in the coming months. We've got to stop them."

"Couldn't you give this Ong Chwee Seng a dual

personality, like you did with Colonel Tee and his son, Jordan?" said Kuan Hee.

"I couldn't do a Jekyll and Hyde on Ong Chwee Seng then. They were suspicious of me. They suspected I had tampered with Colonel Tee's operation five years ago. They also had your mother. I was afraid for her safety," said Professor Wang.

"He's even more ruthless now, Dad," said Kuan Hee. "His men kill in cold blood. They don't care a damn about human life."

"That's what the Brigadier has been telling me too," said Professor Wang. "Son, I am too old. I don't have the strength or stamina to fight for the country. But you can—stand up to them, for Singapore's sake."

"What should I do, Dad?" asked Kuan Hee.

"Go back. Gather your friends and other like-minded Singaporeans. Get them to support the opposition parties. Join in their activities. Rouse the public into action. Together, you all can be a veritable force the regime has to reckon with," said Professor Wang.

"Will I be up to it?" asked Kuan Hee.

"You can, if you put your mind to it," said Professor Wang. "Don't worry about your mother. I'll convince her. In these difficult times, we have to put country before self."

"I will try my best, Dad," said Kuan Hee.

"One more thing, Kuan Hee," said Professor Wang. "Colonel Tee forced me to work on reproductive cloning of human beings. He wants to create a new race of elite individuals. He wants these clones to inhabit the country in the future. He says Singapore has no place for laggards."

"Laggards?" said Kuan Hee.

"Yes, that's the term he used for people who can't make it to university," said Professor Wang.

"But he was an 'A' level holder. He didn't go to university!" said Kuan Hee.

"Apparently, he has forgotten this or he has gotten

over his inferiority complex. The few times that I met him, he rambled on about how the elite could change the face of Singapore," said Professor Wang. "He wanted me to create an assembly line for cloning human beings. He actually believed the clones could form the new pure race of Singapore, that they would eventually become the ruling race of Singapore."

"You mean, replace the four official races that we now have?" said Kuan Hee.

"Not replace, son," said Professor Wang. "It's going to be the fifth race—and the dominant one."

"That is a preposterous proportion, Dad," said Kuan Hee.

"I know it is a load of bull, but Colonel Tee doesn't," said Professor Wang. "My guess is—since he is no longer human, he wants to create a whole tribe of non-humans like him to populate the island. That way, he won't be a freak."

"We have got to expose him, Dad," said Kuan Hee.

"Son, I have a job for you," said Professor Wang. "Destroy the memory bank. It will put an end to his nonsense."

"Where's the memory bank?" asked Kuan Hee.

"He's hidden it somewhere," said Professor Wang. "It's mobile. It's on a computer. He keeps moving it around."

"How do I find it?" asked Kuan Hee.

"I have placed a tracker on it," said Professor Wang. "It's a robot caterpillar."

"A robot caterpillar?" said Kuan Hee. "I didn't know you had a robot caterpillar."

"Yes, son," said Professor Wang. "It's hiding in the CPU of the computer. They were watching me all the time I was working at the computer. So my only choice was to get a robot caterpillar to crawl inside when no one was looking. You can locate it using the robot housefly's remote control. It's on the same frequency. Have you got the remote with you? I will show you how."

"It's in my backpack," said Kuan Hee.

"Later then," said Professor Wang. "My plan is for you to use the two robots Alex and Xander. Blast the entire computer to kingdom come. That will do a clean job."

"Won't Colonel Tee have made copies of the memory bank?" asked Kuan Hee.

"His men do not have the skills," said Professor Wang. "And I only made a master copy. I have not made any other copies. It's too complicated. There are so many trillions of sequences to map. We still do not have the technology to replicate these sequences in one go. One mistake and the data could be corrupted, rendering the memory bank useless."

That evening, Kuan Hee told Lina what the Brigadier and his father had discussed with him. She was shocked to learn Colonel Tee was alive, that Colonel Tee and Ong Chwee Seng were the same person. He showed Lina the note the Brigadier had given him.

"What is it saying?" she asked.

"That Colonel Tee is using the law and the courts to torment the people and keep himself in power," said Kuan Hee. "Remember—he got rid of the judges and replaced them with computer judges. These machines will do his bidding without question." Then he paused. Seeing the confusion in Lina's eyes, he continued.

"In a democracy, there are three separate entities: the executive, the legislative and the judiciary—meaning the Cabinet, the members of parliament and the court judges. Each entity acts as a check on the other two, so there is a balance of power in the government," said Kuan Hee. "However, in Singapore under the Green Party government, all three entities are actually one. Ong Chwee Seng controls all three pillars of government. That's why he can be so ruthless, yet nobody can stop him."

"How can we stop him if others can't?" asked Lina.

"We gather others—the university alumni," said Kuan

Hee. "Remember the Singapore River protest five years ago? We can get these people back. Just spread the word to the alumni."

"So you are going to lead them?" said Lina.

"Guess I have to," said Kuan Hee. "Dad also wants me to destroy the memory bank."

"Why can't the Brigadier get his men to destroy the memory bank?" asked Lina.

"Because, it's none of their business. It's we Singaporeans who have got to save our country from the claws of tyranny," said Kuan Hee. "We can't very well rely on others to do it for us."

"Yah *hor*," said Lina. "Makes sense."

"Of course *lah*, dear," said Kuan Hee.

CHAPTER 23

The Brigadier presented Professor Wang and Mrs Wang with United States diplomatic passports, for the Professor was doing top-secret work for the United States government. The couple was to fly off to Fayetteville Regional Airport in North Carolina from Hang Nadim International Airport in Batam. Fort Braggs was about twenty kilometres north of the airport. Kuan Hee and Lina had to say their goodbyes to his parents on the Artemis. Both did not have their passports with them so they could not enter Batam.

Mrs Wang was reluctant to leave Kuan Hee behind. She was afraid he would be in danger if he returned to Singapore. But she knew no amount of persuasion could get Kuan Hee to change his mind. After being apart from his parents for more than a year, Kuan Hee was reunited with them for three weeks. He was sad to part with them again. But he was a big man now, with responsibilities on his shoulder. It was no time for second thoughts. He and Lina bade a teary farewell as his parents boarded a speedboat to take them to Batam, fifteen minutes away from the ship. The pair promised to take little Huei Huei to visit her grandparents in the near future.

Kuan Hee had recovered fully. He and Lina were also due to return to Singapore, but before they set sail, the Brigadier wanted a word with Kuan Hee.

"There's someone I would like you to meet when you return to Singapore," said the Brigadier. "He'll be of great help to you."

"Yes, Mr Walmsley," said Kuan Hee.

"Remember the senior police officer who interviewed you at the Police Cantonment Complex five years ago?" said the Brigadier.

Kuan Hee nodded. "You mean, the Superintendent?" Kuan Hee said.

"He is now a Deputy Commissioner of Police," said the Brigadier. "In fact, he is the Acting Commissioner of Police now that the Police Commissioner has passed away."

"I didn't get his name then," said Kuan Hee.

"DC Tangarajoo," said the Brigadier. "He too thought well of you. Well enough to mention your name to me. He isn't a fan of the Green Party government. On the contrary, he wants to put a stop to the injustice the Green Party government is perpetuating in Singapore."

"Will he help restore democracy in Singapore?" asked Kuan Hee.

"He is trying to find a way," said the Brigadier. "But he can't do it by himself. That's why I spoke to you the other day about doing national service, remember?"

"Yes, Mr Walmsley," said Kuan Hee. "You wanted me to bring together young people to oppose the Green party government."

"Yes, that's it," said the Brigadier. "You were one of the student leaders who led the protest at the Singapore River five years ago. Can you do it again?"

"Yes, Mr Walmsley," said Kuan Hee.

"DC Tangarajoo needs the help of people power to topple Ong Chwee Seng's regime," said the Brigadier.

"You mean, like how the Filipino people got together

to bring down the dictator Ferdinand Marcos in the 1980s?" said Kuan Hee.

"I see, you studied history," said the Brigadier. "The Filipinos took to the streets to protest against election fraud. Some army units joined them in rebelling against the Marcos government. Eventually, people power won."

"Is that how we should overthrow the Ong Chwee Seng government?" asked Kuan Hee.

"In a nutshell, yes," said the Brigadier. "Can you do it, Kuan Hee? For your country, for your people?"

"Yes of course, Mr Walmsley," said Kuan Hee.

"Good. I'll tell DC Tangarajoo the good news then," said the Brigadier. "Here's what you need to do, Kuan Hee."

CHAPTER 24

In the small room above the shophouse in Realty Park, Kuan Hee and Lina spent an afternoon calling their old friends at Temasek University. Kuan Hee also contacted the student leaders of other universities he had got acquainted with five years ago at the Singapore River protest.

"What if some of them play us out?" said Lina. "They might report us to the G."

"We have to take the risk," said Kuan Hee. "You were there with them then. Do they look like people who will do us in?"

"I am only saying—what if," said Lina. "I didn't say they would."

"Don't be paranoid, dear," said Kuan Hee.

"Some of the phone numbers don't work anymore," said Lina.

"We can try reaching these student leaders through the alumni pages of the universities on Facebook. We may have some luck there," said Kuan Hee.

"How many people do you think we can get for the protest," asked Lina.

"Hopefully, maybe 30,000," said Kuan Hee.

"The logistics will be mind-boggling," said Lina.

"We have done it before," said Kuan Hee. "My only worry is money."

"We can borrow some of the stuff like megaphones," said Lina.

"We still need money to buy water; make banners and placards," said Kuan Hee.

"Can we crowdsource?" asked Lina.

"That will give the game away," said Kuan Hee. "If the G finds out, they will swoop down on us before we get a chance to take to the streets."

There was the sound of footsteps in the staircase. Kuan Hee got up to open the door. Tim and Navin came in bearing bags of food and drinks.

"Why so late?" said Kuan Hee.

"The queue at Pizza Hut was long," said Navin. "I don't know why there are so many people buying pizza today."

"It's the end of the month, for goodness's sake," said Lina. "People get their pay and splurge."

"*Wah!* Lina," said Tim. "Smart girl, you." Lina blushed. Tim liked to tease her.

"You look OK, man," said Navin.

"It's the seaview," said Kuan Hee, "and plenty of rest and relaxation."

"So lucky," said Tim. "Fancy spending a month on a ship on the high sea, doing nothing."

"Don't jest, Tim," said Lina. "Kuan Hee was recovering from a bullet wound in the back, you know."

"Seriously, how's the injury?" asked Tim.

Kuan Hee pulled off his T-shirt and showed his friends his back. The wound had healed nicely, but there was a four-centimetre scar left behind by the surgical operation to remove the bullet. Otherwise his back was unmarked.

Navin pressed the scar gently. "It's quite near the heart," he said.

"Missed his heart by two centimetres," said Lina. "That's what the doctor said."

"Yes, the bullet was lodged in the muscles near my heart," said Kuan Hee.

"Lucky chap, real lucky," said Tim.

"That's the third time you have used 'lucky' today, Tim," said Kuan Hee.

"With you around, we seem to be falling into adventure every now and then," said Tim. "When will life return to normalcy?"

"Let's get down to business," said Kuan Hee as Lina opened the food boxes and passed around the pizzas and chicken wings.

"I'll take down the minutes," said Lina.

"Putting together the street protest is going to be a nightmare," said Kuan Hee. "There's a lot of preparation work to do. Like the Singapore River protest, we will have a co-ordinating committee with these four groups: media, logistics, security and manpower. Any takers?"

"I'll take security," said Tim.

"Media," said Navin.

"Lina, you take logistics, OK?" said Kuan Hee. Lian nodded. "I will take manpower."

Kuan Hee described the responsibilities for each of the group. When he had finished, he asked for questions. Lina was the first to put up her hand.

"How am I going to get donations for water and bread?" she asked.

"Put up requests for these items on Facebook, but only after the protest has gone underway," said Kuan Hee. "This way, it will be too late to stop the protest."

"So I set up a new WhatsApp account for information sharing?" said Navin.

"Yes. Use it to update the water, phone charging and first aid locations," said Kuan Hee. "Also, to tell protesters where to get umbrellas—it's going to be hot, and the rain could come anytime."

"You forgot another important use of umbrellas—shield against tear gas canisters and pepper sprays," said Navin.

"Agreed!" said Tim. "And I am worried about people smuggling in a bomb in a bag or something. There are so many entry points in the protest. It won't be easy to check everyone."

"Just keep your eyes out for suspicious characters," said Kuan Hee. "And Navin, weed out all false postings on Facebook. We can't have sinister characters scaring the protesters and creating panic with false messages."

"Who's in charge of picking up the trash?" asked Lina.

"You," said Kuan Hee. "It's under logistics." Lina frowned. "Why so many things under logistics?" she complained.

"Don't worry," said Kuan Hee. "I'll get you able helpers from the alumni."

"Have we got everything covered?" said Tim.

"I have to set up a page for information sharing between the protesters," said Navin.

"Use getforme.com's forums," said Kuan Hee. "They have been around since 1999. People trust them. Their moderators will keep an eye on the postings. Give you less work—no need to monitor the postings."

"We will run out of money pretty quickly," said Lina. "There won't be enough to sustain the protest."

"Just hope the public will help," said Kuan Hee, "like they did five years ago. Once we have got a critical mass of protesters, the donations will come pouring in. I'm sure."

"What about the memory bank, Kuan Hee?" asked Lina. "You promised your father you would destroy it."

"I am leaving it on the backburner," said Kuan Hee. "The street protest is more important. We must get Ngoh Shi Ping and the others released first. The by-elections are looming."

"I have created the WhatsApp, Facebook and getforme.com accounts," said Navin, looking up from his

MacBook. "And on channelsingapore.com, there is a news article about the detained opposition leaders."

"Where?" Lina asked. "Turn the screen—I can't see from where I am."

"It says Ngoh Shi Ping is suspected to be involved in a conspiracy to harm Singapore," said Tim, summarizing the article. "It seems the Ong Chwee Seng government is pointing an accusing finger at a foreign government. But it has not named the foreign government."

"Anything on Tan Eng Chai?" asked Kuan Hee.

"It says here that Tan Eng Chai is being investigated for treason—colluding with Ngoh Shi Ping and a foreign government to overthrow an elected government," said Tim.

"It seems Ong Chwee Seng is getting desperate," said Kuan Hee. "He is adamant about keeping these two out of the by-elections."

"But it's unfair," said Lina. "It's downright dirty."

"Welcome to politics, Lina," said Tim.

"Will they be released in time for the by-elections?" asked Lina.

"Fat hope," said Kuan Hee. "Which is why we are pinning our hopes on the street demonstrations—to force the Green Party government to set the opposition leaders free."

"Kuan Hee, we still haven't decided on the venue for the street protest," said Navin.

"I was about to ask you guys," said Kuan Hee, "for suggestions."

"I'm sure you already have a site in mind, Kuan Hee," said Tim.

"Yes, Singapore River, where we held a protest as university students," said Kuan Hee. "We have done it there before, so we are familiar with the place."

"Also, it would be difficult for the army to use its armored personnel carriers there," said Navin.

"I agree," said Tim. "It's also a tourist attraction. The

army will think twice about using force. Too many eyes on them."

"When is the big day?" asked Lina.

"Next Friday," said Kuan Hee. "We can't wait too long. We have to take the G by surprise."

"OK," said everyone in unison.

CHAPTER 25

Deputy Commissioner of Police Ajay Tangarajoo looked different out of uniform. Promotion had come at a cost to his appearance. He was no longer the stern-looking middle-aged man that Kuan Hee had sat across from in the interview room at the Police Cantonment Complex five years ago. Gone was the sleek black hair he had combed neatly into a curry puff pattern. In its place was a mass of frizzy grey hair, which tried hard to conceal a bald patch on top. But DC Tangarajoo was still using Gatsby haircream—its familiar mild aqua smell was unmistakable in the air around him. And he had the same gruff voice.

"Kuan Hee, I saw something in you five years ago," said DC Tangarajoo. 'I was not wrong. You are a promising young man. I heard your father is a brilliant scientist. I think you will be one too."

"Thank you, Mr Tangarajoo," said Kuan Hee. "I was a little apprehensive about meeting you. But, in civilian clothes, you look very fatherly. I am not so nervous anymore."

DC Tangarajoo smiled. His gold teeth shone under the bright halogen lights of the ToastBox café in CHIJMES.

"James Walmsley says you have something to tell me,"

said DC Tangarajoo. *He must mean the street protest,* Kuan Hee thought. *The Brigadier said he could help me.*

Kuan Hee looked around the café, then at DC Tangarajoo.

"It's alright, Kuan Hee," said DC Tangarajoo. "We aren't speaking in a loud voice. Moreover, everyone here is engaged in conversation. No one will pay attention to what we are saying."

"We are organizing a street protest next Friday," said Kuan Hee. "It's along the Singapore River."

DC Tangarajoo's eyes met Kuan Hee's. "It may not work, Kuan Hee," he said. "The government will not yield." Kuan Hee sank in his chair.

"But, you are welcome to try," said DC Tangarajoo. "Just how many people do you intend to call up?"

"About 30,000," said Kuan Hee.

"That's quite ambitious," said DC Tangarajoo. "It won't be easy keeping order in such a big group. Perhaps, I can help."

"Thank you, Mr Tangarajoo," said Kuan Hee, clasping his hands.

"Keep calm. Don't be alarmed, Kuan Hee," said DC Tangarajoo. "I just want to help smoothen things for you. Let nothing happen that can ruin your event."

"Mr Tangarajoo, my main worry is that the army will send armored personnel carriers to crush our peaceful protest," said Kuan Hee.

"Don't worry, it won't happen," said DC Tangarajoo. "Not if I can help it. Just go ahead."

"Thanks, Mr Tangarajoo," said Kuan Hee.

"You know, these are difficult times for everyone in the country," said DC Tangarajoo. "Some people are hiding behind the law, using it to advance their own selfish causes. And other people who carry out the law are helpless. They can't do anything to stop the first group legally. Do you understand what I am saying, Kuan Hee?"

"Yes, Mr Tangarajoo," said Kuan Hee. He took out the

slip of paper that the Brigadier had given him and placed it on the small table, with the print facing DC Tangarajoo. The Deputy Commissioner of Police glanced at the note.

"Ah yes, you do understand," said DC Tangarajoo. "Kuan Hee, this thing called justice serves not just one side alone. It serves both sides. Justice doesn't protect only the government. It also protects the people. And when one side abuses its trust, the other side can take up arms to protect it, in the same way that justice protects them."

"It's quite a handful you have told me," said Kuan Hee. "I'm trying to fathom the deep meaning behind your words."

"You are a clever chap, Kuan Hee," said DC Tangarajoo. "I am sure you understand what I have just told you. Did you say the protest will take place next Friday?"

"Yes, next Friday along Singapore River," said Kuan Hee.

CHAPTER 26

In its headlines, the local newspapers announced writs of election had been issued. Nomination Day was two days after the planned street protest. It seemed the Green Party government was adamant not to let the Unity Party take part in the by-elections. Perhaps, as DC Tangarajoo had said, the street protest would not result in the release of the Unity Party's leaders in time for the elections. The opposition was doomed to lose the by-elections.

It was against this background that the street protest along Singapore River went ahead. The protest machinery had been cranked up. The volunteers had confirmed their attendance. Water, bread, banners and placards had been requisitioned. Everyone was raring to go. Nothing could stop the planned protest. So the protesters poured into the area around Singapore River.

Facebook postings calling for people to support the protest went viral. Social media was abuzz with excitement. Everyone who came across the posts wanted to come to the Singapore River. They came from all walks of life—the young and the old, the cleaners and the office workers, the able and the differently abled—all coming together with one ultimate purpose in mind, to topple the dictatorship of Ong Chwee Seng. Getting the opposition leaders released was just one of those things that would help the protesters achieve their ultimate goal, so they were for it too.

With the large crowds came the sponsors. Some donated piping hot noodles, some donated water, some donated umbrellas. Soon, more things were being donated than needed. Lina, who was in charge of logistics for the protest had quite a load on her small shoulders.

The police had erected barricades ostensibly to keep protesters reined in, but their real goal was actually to thwart the army's armored personnel carriers.

There was camaraderie among the protesters. Many shared their food and water. They lent their power banks to their fellow protesters. They huddled under shared umbrellas to take shelter from the hot sun.

Singaporeans were supposed to be *kiasu* and *kiasi*, but today, they shed these traits for the common good. They were, perhaps, reprising what their forefathers did when they migrated to Singapore from China, India and other countries, and met in an inhospitable environment—they put aside their differences and got together to build a better future.

Netizens swarmed the protest organisers' online forums to disparate the Green Party government for trampling on the rights of citizens. They shared anecdotes of how the government had come down hard on non-graduates. They also condemned the introduction of newly enacted laws making polygamy legal for graduate men. Navin and his volunteers sat on their backpacks with eyes glued to their MacBook screens. They were busy looking out for false messages meant to cause alarm to the protesters.

The protest was achieving more than what it originally aimed for. People were uniting in adversity. Tim was determined not to let gatecrashing supporters of the Green Party ruin their efforts. He and his security team kept an eagle eye out for these spoilers and spies.

By midday, the crowd had spilled onto the grass verges and the open spaces of nearby office buildings. Everything was proceeding so smoothly that they had all let their guard down. Was this the lull before the storm? Then came the rumbling of heavy vehicles. Then the turrets of the army's armored personnel carriers appeared on one side of Cavenagh Bridge. It was an intimidating presence. It put paid to the protesters' idyllic holiday mood. The roar grew louder as the armored personnel carriers neared the Singapore River. Several drones flew over the protest site. Their silvery blue colour announced their military ownership. These drones became a ubiquitous presence at the Singapore River protest.

On the other side of Cavenagh Bridge, a convoy of dark blue armored carriers roared into view. These belonged to the police. The two rival groups of armored vehicles were now only fifty metres apart on St Andrew's Road, in front of the bridge. They were now facing off each other. It was a tense moment for both groups and the protesters along Singapore River.

Was the situation about to explode into violence? No one knew. Both the army and the police seemed to be wondering which side would blink first.

Kuan Hee's first thoughts were the safety of the protesters. With the armored carriers effectively sealing the Cavenagh Bridge side of the Singapore River, the only means of escape—in case of trouble—was through South Bridge Road, next to Parliament House. Using loudhailers, Tim and his volunteers prepared the protesters to be ready to leave the protest site in an orderly manner.

But some of the protesters were infuriated by the presence of the army's armored personnel carriers. They cajoled others near them to move towards Cavenagh Bridge towards the army vehicles. These protesters had their own leaders now. As they moved into St Andrew's Road, more protesters joined them. Tim's volunteers were helpless; they could not stop the waves of people marching towards the army vehicles.

The presence of protesters around the police armored carriers complicated the situation. Kuan Hee and Tim were worried.

"We've got to get the protesters away from the armored carriers," said Kuan Hee. "It's too dangerous there. The army is ruthless."

Using loudhailers, Kuan Hee and Tim tried to coax the protesters milling around the armored carriers to retreat to the Singapore River.

Just then, a contingent of policemen came up behind the police armored carriers. The policemen kept the protesters behind them, forming a human chain in front of the armored carriers. A red anti-riot vehicle drove up and a senior police officer atop the vehicle ordered the protesters to disperse from the area.

Meanwhile, soldiers were pouring into St Andrew's Road, behind the army's armored personnel carriers. They had their rifles at the ready.

It was indeed a standoff in the making. The minutes ticked by uneventfully. The afternoon heat made standing in the sun unbearable for all parties. Lina's mobile water stations were a welcome respite for the protesters and the policemen who took generous swigs of the liquid.

Kuan Hee, Tim and Navin were now standing next to a police armored carrier, pondering their next move, as the setting sun prepared to make way for the darkness of evening.

"So, do we stay put?" asked Tim.

"Might as well make full use of the situation," said Navin. "With the police protecting us, I am sure the army will think twice about crushing our protest."

"It's your call, Kuan Hee," said Tim.

Kuan Hee combed the back of his hair with his fingers. "We stay for the night," he told them.

Soon the skies above the Singapore River were pitch-black. Instead of thinning, the mass of protesters crept across both sides of the river as youngsters heading outdoors for a weekend of fun joined in the protest. The river glistened as a sea of candlelights and flashlights lit up the promenades alongside the river as far as the eye could see. There had to be at least 50,000 people gathering by the river tonight. They were a formidable force to reckon with.

The four friends had ensconced themselves in the open space next to Cavenagh Bridge. They were seated on the bare concrete screed, having a powwow. Metres away stood the police armored carriers and their attendants.

"Darkness is when the enemy will be most likely to take action," said Kuan Hee. "They may come in when we least expect. Navin, tell everyone to keep an eye out for intruders." Navin typed furiously on his MacBook.

"The army drones have been hovering over us the whole day," said Tim. "They must know we are the organisers."

"Here they come again," said Lina. Two drones were now flying overhead.

"They can't beat our little Busy," said Lina. "No one notices little Busy."

"We may be the army's target," said Kuan Hee.

"Which is why we are sitting here, next to the police armored carriers," said Tim. "The soldiers have to deal with the police too, if they come after us."

"Smart move," said Navin.

"Look! The soldiers are pitching tents on the Padang," said Tim, as the hammering of metal pierced the night in the City Hall area. "There must be at least a dozen of them."

CHAPTER 27

The army commandoes came in the dead of the night. They climbed up the embankment and hid below the Cavenagh Bridge. It had to be just before dawn. It was that time of the morning when even the most alert of men would doze off, yielding to the lure of the cool morning breeze and their dreams.

Kuan Hee awoke with a start. There was cold metal pressing against his throat. Lina stirred beside him. Two men, in aquasuits dripping wet, were squatting in front of him. Tim and Navin were on duty, prowling along the promenade. The policemen were so near, and yet so far away. Kuan Hee dared not let out a cry; Lina's safety was paramount in his mind. He let the figures grab his arms and lead him away.

The three figures were at the edge of the Singapore River when Lina let out a shrill cry. It broke the silence of the night. She had awoken with a start. The river water had seeped through her shorts and she was now wet underneath. She ran after the men, screaming at the top of her voice. Tim and Navin were too far away to be of help. Some policemen gave chase but it was too late. The two commandoes had whisked Kuan Hee away in a rubber dinghy waiting in the water.

Lina and the policemen could only watch helplessly as the boat sped into the darkness. Soon Cavenagh Bridge was a hive of activity. The protesters learnt of the kidnapping and were anxious. The protest was now without a head. It was rudderless. Fortunately, Tim rose to the occasion. He got the volunteers together and made known to them he was in charge till Kuan Hee returned. He implemented a duty roster for the volunteers to keep watch on the river. In their plan for the security of the protest, Kuan Hee and his team had provided for precautions to take in case of a land attack by the soldiers. Never in their mind did it occur to them that the army would use commandoes to deal with them using stealth boats. After all, they were just ordinary protesters.

It was dawn when the protesters settled down. Tim, Navin and Lina sat down to discuss a plan for saving Kuan Hee.

"He's got little Busy with him," said Lina. "We can track him using GPS." She unfolded the remote control card and activated the locate feature. At once, a map of the Singapore River appeared on the screen. A little red dot beeped continually on the screen.

"He's nearby," said Tim. "They didn't go far. Zoom in on the co-ordinates."

"Little Busy is in The Float@Marina," said Lina. "Kuan Hee must be in there somewhere."

"We have to get to him straightaway," said Tim, "before they move him elsewhere. By then it will be too late."

"Someone needs to take charge here," said Navin. "But you and I have to go. Who can do the job?"

"I am going too," said Lina.

"Nope, Lina. You can't go. It's too dangerous," said Tim. "Just stay put and wait for news." Lina knew it was futile to argue with Tim. She realised she would be putting the two men in danger if she went along.

"Who's in charge while you two are gone?" Lina asked.

"You," said Tim.

"But I can't," said Lina. "I am not up to it."

"It's only for an hour or two," said Tim. "Besides it will give you something to keep busy while we are away."

Lina handed the remote to Tim. She took out AleXander the robots and Navin placed them in his backpack.

"AleXander will be enough," said Tim. "Their combined firepower can punch a hole through the enemy."

"Here, bring along Tizzy too," said Lina, placing the robot dragonfly and its remote in Tim's hands.

The two men waved goodbye and made their way through the protesters. They had to take a circuitous route to Raffles Avenue, for the soldiers had blocked off the City Hall area.

Sitting in front of The Float@Marina was a 30,000-seat gallery. It was specially built to host National Day parades. The seating gallery was a simple concrete structure consisting of a hundred-metre-wide concrete stairway tall enough to hold eighty rows of seats. On top sat a reception hall, about seven metres long. Behind the seating gallery was an open-air car park partially shielded from the elements by the slanting gallery structure.

Tim and Navin stood behind a pillar outside Marina Square. From there, they had a clear view of Raffles Avenue in front of them and beyond it, the rear of The Float@Marina.

"The car park looks deserted," said Navin. "The soldiers are congregated on the Padang. Looks like nobody is here. But looks can be deceiving."

"The only enclosed space in the seating gallery is the reception hall on top. The soldiers should be holding Kuan Hee in there," said Tim. "But we can't see from here. It's all walled up."

"Let's make sure," said Navin. He opened little Busy's

remote control and pressed the locate button. "Kuan Hee's still in the building."

"Fly little Busy; take a look at Kuan Hee," said Tim.

Little Busy peeped out of Kuan Hee's pocket. It flitted around him. Kuan Hee was leaning against the wall, staring blankly into space. He seemed to be deep in thought. His hands were behind him, fastened together with plastic cable ties. About three metres away, two men in black were having their breakfast at a wooden table. They wore their pistol strapped under their shoulder. At another table, another man was doing work at a notebook computer. He had his back facing Kuan Hee. There was nobody else in the longish room.

"Fly it to Kuan Hee's ear," said Tim. Navin tabbed on the remote screen and little Busy buzzed near Kuan Hee's ear.

"Navin and I are across the road, outside Marina Square," Tim's voice came through little Busy's speakers. "Tilt your head if you can hear me." Kuan Hee lowered his head slightly; he had woken from his thoughts. His eyes were gleaming. He flashed a weak smile.

"We are coming to get you," said Tim. "Hold tight." Kuan Hee nodded. Tim and Navin were indeed brave. They were unarmed, yet undaunted by their perilous task.

"Ready, Navin?" asked Tim.

"Hold on a second," said Navin. He reached into his pocket for his cigarettes. "Let me take a puff first."

"Later, *lah*," said Tim. "We'll do fine. Don't worry."

Tim and Navin ran across Raffles Avenue to the underside of the seating gallery. There was a lone unmarked van in the car park. Tim placed his hand on its hood. It was cold. The van had been there for at least an hour. There was a lift near the van. Navin pointed to the camera on a pillar.

"The soldiers came here at short notice. I don't think they have access to the CCTV," said Tim. "We take the risk."

"They must have used this lift to go up to the reception hall," said Navin. "The door adjacent to the lift could be the staircase."

"Let's find out," said Tim. Both men moved stealthily into the staircase. There was another door opposite. Navin took a look through a small window slot in it.

"It leads to the floating platform," said Navin. "No one outside." Tim looked up the staircase. There were eight landings.

"The reception hall must be on the fourth level," said Tim. He gave the thumbs-up gesture and they climbed the stairs.

At the top of the staircase, a door opened into an enclosed lift lobby. *There is no one guarding the lobby.* Tim told himself. *These guys are overconfident. They must be thinking no one will ever know they are here. They have forgotten technology works wonders.*

Tim and Navin sidled into the lobby. There was a camera observing their every move, but the two men ignored its presence. There was a pair of doors on one side of the lobby. *It probably leads to the hall.* Tim told himself. Both men took turns to peep through the window slot in the door.

There were the same two men they had seen on the remote screen. They seemed to be in conversation. The third man was still at his table. Kuan Hee was nowhere in sight.

"He must be on the other side of this wall," Tim told Navin. He gave Navin the thumbs-up gesture. *For their own convenience, the soldiers had parked themselves and Kuan Hee next to the lift lobby,* Tim thought. *These guys are either truly unprofessional or utterly complacent. But I thought they are commandoes.*

At once, Navin released AleXander the robots from the confined space of the backpack. He opened their front panels. They were now primed to use their weapon systems. Both robots had been programmed to recognize both men's voices and act on their verbal instructions.

Stunt-hurt-hit-destroy, Tim repeated the commands to himself. The robots would act on these commands to fire their weapons. Tim gestured to Navin to stay behind the door while he entered the room. Xander stood at Navin's heels. His rockets were too powerful to be used this time. He was on standby, for use only as a last resort.

At once, Tim opened the door and rolled on the floor towards where Kuan Hee was sitting. Alex the robot ran into the room and stood ready to fire his laser weapon system. It had the three men locked in its sights. Taken by surprise, the three men drew their pistols, but before they could open fire Tim had shouted 'stunt-fire-3' to Alex.

The electrolaser unit in Alex's laser arsenal shot a powerful electric current at each of the three men in succession. It worked the same way a Taser electroshock gun worked. The electric currents incapacitated the three men instantly. They fell to the ground, writhing in agony. Alex's arsenal was indeed formidable.

Tim had enough time to snatch Kuan Hee to safety. The three friends had a three-minute headstart. Together with the robots, they scrambled down the staircase, not once looking back.

CHAPTER 28

The protesters leaning near the police armored carriers were getting restless by mid-morning. They were preparing to march towards City Hall where the army armored personnel carriers were stationed. Lina and her fellow volunteers could only watch helplessly as the protesters veered off the promenade onto St Andrew's Road.

It was then that Kuan Hee, Tim and Navin arrived breathless at Cavenagh Bridge. Were they in time to stop the protesters from committing suicide?

Kuan Hee took to the loudhailer to calm the protesters. He asked for restrain. Thinking quickly, he jogged their memories of the army's brutal excesses five years ago. Giving a blow-by-blow graphic recount of the army's crackdown on protesters just metres away from where they were standing, he managed to instill fear in their eyes. They viewed the army's armored personnel carriers in different light.

The four friends heaved a sigh of relief. They had averted a disastrous situation—but for how long, it was anybody's guess. It would only take a little poking from a partisan fellow protester to rekindle their rage.

Meanwhile, Lina clung close to Kuan Hee. She had a

million things to tell him, but all these had to wait. Pressing matters of national concern took first place today.

By noon, the police presence along Cavenagh Bridge had grown in tandem with the crowd of protesters. Now, there were Gurkhas in their midst. The policemen were also better equipped today; they were helmeted and carried shields.

Perhaps, it was the heat of the afternoon. The crowd on this second day of the protest had dwindled to about 20,000 people, but it was still large enough to make an impact. Kuan Hee and his team decided that the protesters would march from South Bridge Road to North Bridge Road and Victoria Street instead. They were heading for the Istana, the President's official residence.

The protesters were hungry for action after a morning of inactivity. They knocked on drums, sang nostalgic national songs such as 'Stand Up for Singapore' and rattled sticks in the air. They waved their banners and placards as they moved along the city's thoroughfares. Traffic had slowed to a crawl. Kuan Hee, Lina, Tim and Navin led the march with Alex and Xander the robots walking in front of Kuan Hee. Although he hated for the world to know of the robots' existence, he had no choice. He could not risk being caught by the G operatives again.

At the main intersections of the roads, policemen in riot gear stood watching the procession, but did nothing to stop it. There were no signs of the soldiers along the protest route so far. The army's armored personnel carriers were still parked along St Andrew's Road, facing off with the police's armored carriers.

It had to happen. At the junction of Victoria Street and Bras Basah Road, a convoy of infantry fighting vehicles rumbled into view. Atop their turrets were soldiers who trained their machine guns at the procession of protesters approaching the junction. The soldiers were determined not to let the protesters pass. It was another faceoff in the making.

No sooner had the army's armored personnel carriers taken up positions, then some dark-blue armored carriers pulled up at the same junction from Bras Basah Road. There were Gurkhas manning the machine guns atop the turrets. Behind them was a special operations command vehicle and several armored multi-purpose patrol vehicles. These belonged to the Gurkha police contingent, which had been around since 1949. It had a fierce reputation for strictness and loyalty.

Suddenly it looked as if the police were intentionally creating a head-to-head confrontation with the army. The stakes for control of Singapore had gone up. The Ong Chwee Seng government now had its hands full. Would the Prime Minister order his army into street battles against the police? It would effectively be civil war if he did! It would also plunge Singapore into chaos.

The kilometre-long procession by now was within metres of the junction.

"Looks like the police are on our side," said Tim.

"The police are indeed taking to the streets to revolt against the Ong Chwee Seng government," said Kuan Hee. "We have a fighting chance to overthrow the military regime."

"If civil war erupts, it would be years before we know which side has won," said Navin. "I am not joking."

"Do we turn back, Kuan Hee?" asked Lina.

"We go back to the last junction and turn into Stamford Road. From there to Orchard Road," said Kuan Hee. He was not giving up his plan to lead the protesters to the Istana.

The four friends waded through the thick crowd and arrived outside Capitol Building at the junction of North Bridge Road and Stamford Road. There, they waved the protesters on to Stamford Road.

The sun was now high above the protesters. The umbrellas were not much help in deflecting the heat. The protesters had just passed the Presbyterian Church and were about to turn into the bottom of Orchard Road. Their stomachs were growling for attention. It was time for them to take a break. But they were only a hundred metres away from their destination; they trudged on at the behest of Kuan Hee and his team.

At last, the procession crept to the gate of the Istana. Kuan Hee and his team heaved a sigh of relief. They had seen only policemen along this last part of the march; except for the Istana ceremonial guards, there were no soldiers in sight. The traffic along upper Orchard Road had come to a stop at the junction before the Istana. Policemen diverted the vehicles away from the protesters. A score of policemen formed a human chain across the Istana entrance.

The protest volunteers set up water stations opposite the gates, next to the Istana Gardens. They distributed boxes of noodles and sandwiches to the voracious protesters. The donors were generous to the cause and the protesters were well fed.

Kuan Hee and his team set up base across the road from the Istana. Navin typed away on his MacBook. He was getting status reports from other parts of the procession whose tail trailed to the YMCA Building in Stamford Road.

"Strange! The other reporting centres are saying the soldiers are nowhere near," said Navin.

"They aren't here too," said Kuan Hee. "Could they be preparing to hit us in one fell swoop?"

"Too bad we left no one at Singapore River, otherwise we can get news on the armored personnel carriers there," said Tim.

"Anything on the local news Websites?" asked Kuan Hee. After some minutes, Navin looked up and shook his head.

"Keep trying, Navin," said Kuan Hee. "Something is up. I can feel it in my bones."

Then Kuan Hee, Lina and Tim walked down the road,

past MacDonald's House to Cathay Building. From the front of Cathay Cinema, they had a clear view of the whole stretch of Bras Basah Road up to Raffles Hotel. The traffic was flowing smoothly. The junction at Raffles Hotel was no longer barricaded. The army's armored personnel carriers were nowhere to be seen, so too the Gurkha's armored carriers.

"It's strange," said Kuan Hee, "very strange."

Lina and Tim knew Kuan Hee was now in deep thought. It would be many minutes before he woke from his thoughts. They could only wait patiently. Tim and Lina surfed the Internet on their phones, looking for every piece of news they could find on their protest and trying to locate the soldiers who had been stalking them the past few days.

Then it came. There was breaking news on channelsingapore.com. The Website was exploding with news all of a sudden. The headlines read:

Police Revolt Against Government

There was a blow-by-blow account of the police revolt, which was taking place at several places in Singapore. Police contingents were now attacking the army's infantry regiments at Bedok, Clementi and Bukit Panjang Camps. Over at Kranji and Keat Hong Camps, police armored carriers were engaged in a firefight with the army's armored regiments. And members of the police's Special Tactics and Rescue units were descending on the army commandoes at Hendon Camp.

In a retaliatory move, the army had sent its Leopard main battle tanks to attack the police headquarters at New Phoenix Park in Irrawaddy Road. A news presenter said the Leopard tanks had come up from Balestier Hill Secondary School, behind the police headquarters, and blasted the twin towers of the complex. Numerous injuries were reported at the site of the attack. In a subsequent update, the news presenter reported that the Gurkha police contingent's armored carriers had come racing to the rescue. There was now an intense firefight at the police headquarters. The story was still developing.

"Looks like war has erupted between the police and the army," said Tim.

"The police are no match for the army's Leopard tanks," said Navin. "The tanks can crush them like paper."

"Still too early to say," said Tim. "Don't forget the police's Gurkha contingent. They are a formidable force to reckon with. They go for blood."

"Guys! Breaking news—some Leopard tanks enroute to the Istana," said Navin. "ETA twenty minutes."

"*Wah!* That's too soon," said Tim. "There won't be time to make a getaway if we dillydally."

"We can't fight tanks!" said Lina. "The soldiers have armor protecting them. We only have skin protecting us."

"Don't fret. We've got Alex and Xander the robots," Kuan Hee reminded his friends. Xander can blow a hole through the Leopards."

"Still, we've got to prepare the protesters ahead," said Tim. "We can't take chances with their lives."

"I agree," said Kuan Hee.

"Another update coming up," said Navin. "Boy, these updates are coming fast and furious." The four friends watched a news presenter on channelsingapore.com deliver a live report on the police revolt.

The news presenter said that the police elite units had overrun the infantry regiments at Bedok and Clementi Camps. There was new fighting at Dieppe Barracks in Yishun. She also reported the police headquarters was still under siege, with a fierce battle being fought there.

"Many protesters are leaving," said Navin. "They are going home. These protesters fear for their families. The other centres can't stop them."

"Don't," said Kuan Hee. He had a change of mind suddenly. "The situation is dire. Civil war has erupted. I think it's best we disband the protest. There's no knowing what the army will do. I'm sure they are mad now. Navin, give the instruction to disband."

"OK," said Navin. Tim took to the loudhailer. He thanked the protesters and told them to go home. Before he could finish talking, the protesters were already disappearing in different directions. They too had heard the news of the police revolt.

The MRT trains and buses were packed with people. They were all trying to reach home before it was too late— soldiers were bound to fan out across the island to patrol the streets. There was no telling what these soldiers would do to people still loitering in the streets. Everyone was fearful for his or her life. The good life was about to dissipate. What would the coming days bring to Singapore residents? Nobody could hazard a guess.

When the last of the protesters had left, the four friends crowded into Lina's brother's van and headed home. *Thank goodness Hougang is not a battle scene,* they all thought. *Not yet anyway.*

Along the way, they saw people scurrying through the streets, shops putting up shutters, and shoppers lugging heavy bags of groceries. There was fear in the air. The van did not meet with soldiers during its journey; the soldiers were busy defending their turf across the island.

What a stark contrast in just a few hours! Kuan Hee thought. *This morning, the army seemed to be on top of the situation. Now, their existence is being threatened.*

"Bedok Camp has fallen," said Navin. His MacBook screen shone in the dark interior as it rested on his lap. "The army commanders are frantically looking for men. They are calling up the reservists using Open Mobilisation."

"No use. People are telling their friends on WhatsApp and Facebook to ignore the mobilization exercise," said Tim, taking his eyes off his smartphone to look at the others in the back of the van.

"Let's hope this revolt gathers momentum," said Kuan Hee, keeping his fingers crossed.

"Clementi Camp has been taken too," said Navin.

"The police has the element of surprise going for them," said Tim. "Of course, these two camps will be the first to go. Going forward, it will be difficult to gauge. Once the army collects itself, it will hit back and hard too."

"The army can only depend on the regulars," said Kuan Hee. "How many regulars are there now, Navin?"

Navin scoured the Internet for information on the Singapore army. "According to this US Website, active strength total: 72,000 and reserve strength: 432,000," said Navin.

"Active strength includes those serving national service," said Tim. "So we deduct about 20,000—the annual live births for males. This leaves 52,000 regulars."

"What about the police numbers?" Kuan Hee asked.

"Let's see. Wikipedia has this figure: 38,000," said Navin.

"*Wah!* The army outnumbers the police by 14,000," exclaimed Lina.

"The army also has stronger firepower that the police is hard put to match," said Tim.

"Breaking news again. Soldiers from Amoy Quee and Selarang Camps are on the move," said Navin. "But nothing on their destination."

"They have to or they'll be sitting ducks," said Tim.

"It's one big mess," said Kuan Hee. "Life in the late 2010s was so peaceful." He was reminiscing his childhood days.

"Yeah, I remember everyone in Singapore coming together to celebrate SG50," said Lina. "I was in primary three then."

"I never thought we would come to this," said Navin. "Instead of moving ahead as a people, we now *gostan.*"

Certainly, Singapore residents were a hapless lot in the 2030s, falling from one dictatorship into another. But if they had the never-say-die spirits of these four friends too, there was hope yet for the country.

Back in Realty Park, the four friends huddled on the floor in the small room. They were eager for every bit of news that the online Websites and social media threw up on the police revolt. The videos on Facebook were more revealing of the situation than the news channels. Some pro-government news media were selectively providing information on the revolt. The four friends viewed the top videos trending on singaporehappenings.com. Whether shot from the corridors of high-rise buildings, from the roadside, from behind perimeter chain-link fences, or from moving vehicles, together they provided a bird's eye view of the battles being fought for control of Singapore. Citizen reporting was indeed a veritable tool to fight the government's giant fake news machinery.

"The international community is commenting on the police revolt," said Navin. He scrolled down the breaking news on the sidebar of a news Website for the others to read.

> The United States government urges return to democractic process. It calls for restrain on both sides.

> Britain supports peaceful resolution to the conflict.

> China calls for talks to resolve internal differences in Singapore.

> Japan calls for calm in Singapore conflict.

> Thailand urges both parties to exercise restrain.

> Indonesia calls upon the warring parties to avoid aggravating the situation.

"What about Malaysia and Brunei?" asked Lina.

"Nothing so far," said Navin.

"Both governments must be caught in a spot," said Tim. "Maybe they are waiting for things to become clearer before they say their piece."

"Sitting on the fence?" said Lina.

"A special announcement is being telecast on the official news channel now," said Navin. He turned up the volume on his MacBook.

> The government takes a serious view of the provocations by elements of the police force. It urges the leaders of the unauthorized movement to halt the illegal acts against a popularly elected government. Hostile actions violate our democratic principles, upon which the foundations of our country rest.
>
> The government hereby orders all police units to return to their barracks immediately. Failure to do so will result in severe disciplinary consequences. Leaders of the police revolt are commanded to surrender to the government immediately.
>
> All citizens are reminded of their duty to support the government in its efforts to stabilize the situation in the country.

"Bullshit! Look how they sugarcoat their words," said Tim. "Makes the police look real bad."

"Trying to hookwink us citizens," said Kuan Hee. "They must think we are three-year-old kids."

"Guys, they are just putting on a show for the world to see," said Navin. "Everyone knows it's a load of rubbish."

"What's the situation at New Phoenix Park?" asked

Kuan Hee.

"Two gaping holes on the sides of the twin towers. Thirty-eight dead. The battle's still being waged. Looks like a stand-off between the Gurkhas' armored carriers and the Leopard tanks," said Navin.

"The Gurkhas are a truly amazing force," said Tim. "Truly dependable and loyal. We need more like them." The others nodded in unison. Indeed the Gurkhas were the country's saviour in these tumultuous times.

"So what do we do now?" asked Lina. "Wait?"

"We can't," said Kuan Hee. "We move on. Right now, we must destroy the master tapes, which hold Colonel Tee's memories. Without them, he can't replicate himself like he does now."

"The police still needs us to protest in the streets," said Tim. "We can't just let them fight the army alone."

"Yes, I agree, Tim," said Kuan Hee. He turned his eyes on Tim. "I suggest you lead the protesters. I'll find and destroy the memory bank."

"Good idea," said Navin. "Tim and I can take care of the street demonstrations."

"What you say to this arrangement?" said Kuan Hee.

"OK. But can you handle Colonel Tee alone?" asked Tim.

"I've got AleXander the robots. They are enough," said Kuan Hee.

"And me too," chipped in Lina.

CHAPTER 29

That evening, Tim went to spend the night at Navin's home. News on the police revolt was still trickling in, but both men were too exhausted to keep their eyes peeled for it. Their brains were overworked. They could not process what new information was coming in. Sleep was what they urgently needed.

Kuan Hee and Lina finally got their precious moments alone in the small room.

"Kuan Hee, when you were kidnapped, I was so afraid they would do horrid things to you."

"Yes, dear."

"Were you tortured at The Float@Marina?"

"No, dear."

"Kuan Hee, you are not listening to what I'm saying."

"I am, dear."

"But you are not looking at me."

"I'm tired, dear."

"You weren't tired when you and Tim were running around The Float@Marina with the two robots."

"OK, dear. I'm listening, really." He turned his head to look at her eyes. They twinkled beside his face in the faint ambient light. In them he saw a glowing hunger. Lina flashed a mischievous smile.

"You are wicked."

"I know."

At once, she climbed over him and pressed her body against his. She was breathing heavily. He knew he had to fulfill her immediate needs.

The couple ignored the hard floor beneath them as they wrapped themselves around each other and entered each other's worlds. Relishing their fantasies together was their way of partaking in a sorely needed respite from the mundane world. It was a long night, but much too short for their liking.

It was early afternoon when the pair woke. It was Kuan Hee who was shaken out of slumber by the ringing of his smartphone. He groped for his smartphone on the floor next to him. It was Tim on the line. He had grabbed his forty winks and was on the Internet surfing for tidbits of information on the police revolt the whole morning.

"The Gurkhas have repelled the Leopard tanks," said Tim. Kuan Hee sat up at once.

"It's good news," said Kuan Hee. "Jolly good news."

"The Gurkhas braved the machine guns atop the tanks and launched TOW anti-tank missiles on them," said Tim.

"They sure are a fighting machine," said Kuan Hee. "How did they manage to get their hands on the US-made anti-tank missiles?"

"Search me," said Tim. "Must be the Americans, I guess."

"When did this happen?" asked Kuan Hee.

"At the crack of dawn," said Tim. "But the news only came in just now."

"Can you find out how they have divided the island?" said Kuan Hee. "For our own safety, we can only protest in police-protected areas."

"OK," said Tim. "I am with Navin now."

"Where are you guys?" asked Kuan Hee.

"In his study," said Tim.

"Lina and I will hop over later," said Kuan Hee.

After a late lunch, Kuan Hee and Lina flagged down an Uber taxi along Upper Serangoon Road. They were expecting roadblocks along the way to Sengkang, but fortunately it was an uneventful ride. Hougang had not been marked as an army or police zone yet. They did pass some police minibuses packed with policemen racing through the streets in Sengkang.

Navin lived with his mother in a four-roomed HDB flat in Sengkang, north of Hougang. His father passed away five years ago. His elder brother had moved to a new flat in Punggol when he got married so there was an extra room available. Navin had turned it into his study. It was where Tim and Navin were camped the whole day today.

"Auntie!" Kuan Hee and Lina greeted Navin's mother in unison. She broke into a broad smile as she opened the gate to let them in and then went back to the kitchen to continue her cooking. The heady smell of fish curry permeated the air as the pair entered Navin's study.

The couple threw themselves onto the large cushions on the ceramic floor. Navin resumed the commentary on the police revolt that he had been giving Tim.

"As far as we know, the police have got control of the downtown area, Geylang, Bedok, MacPherson, Serangoon, Hougang," said Navin. "The army controls Changi, Tampines, Jurong, Yishun and Woodlands—especially the outlying areas."

"This means the causeway in Woodlands leading to Johor Bahru, the Tuas Second Link connecting to Tanjung Kupang in Johor, and Changi Airport are under the army's control," said Kuan Hee.

"Effectively, all routes into and out of Singapore are blocked by the army," said Tim.

"Except the harbour," Navin corrected him.

"Oh yeah, I forgot about the harbour," said Tim.

"What if the navy blockades the harbour?" asked Lina.

"The police have got the coastguard," said Kuan Hee. "But their vessels won't be of much use against the navy's destroyers."

"We can only hope the navy won't get involved in the fight," said Tim. "So far the navy and the air force have remained neutral."

"I'm sure their top brass aren't happy about Colonel Tee taking charge of the armed forces," said Kuan Hee. "They are torn between duty and allegiance—duty to their superiors and allegiance to the country. They are merely biding their time now."

"Will the police be able to convince the navy and the air force to take their side?" asked Lina.

"Hard to say," said Kuan Hee. "They need a push. We can push them. The people of Singapore can push them over to the police's side."

"You mean our protest?" said Tim. Kuan Hee nodded.

"Now where would be a good place to stage a protest?" asked Navin. Any suggestions?"

"Must fulfill these conditions: safe, easy to access, maximum exposure," said Kuan Hee.

"How about Chinatown? Along New Bridge Road?" said Tim. "The Police Cantonment Complex is nearby. It's in the middle of town and many people frequent the place, expecially tourists."

"Mmm. The whole stretch of road is wide enough to hold a large procession," said Navin. "The overhead bridge between People's Park Complex and Chinatown is suitable for a look-out station—to spot soldiers."

"It's within the police protected zone. The army won't get in easily," said Kuan Hee. "Any objections?"

None of the four friends voiced disagreement to the suggestion. Just then, the aroma of whole-wheat flour being toasted on the griddle wafted into the study. Soon, Navin's mother appeared at the doorway. In her hands were a plate of chapati and a bowl of fish curry. Lina stretched her hands to receive them. Before she could lay them on the desk, the men had snatched some chapatti from the plate. They were indeed famished. Navin's mother certainly knew how to make delectable chapatis.

"It's set then, New Bridge Road it is," said Kuan Hee. The others nodded in unison. With the chapatis happily devoured, the four friends hunkered down to discuss the protest details.

CHAPTER 30

Colonel Tee's ability to live in another's mind depended on the master tapes hosting his memories. It was Kuan Hee's job to locate the memory bank carrying these tapes and destroy it. Now was the right time to carry out the task. Kuan Hee recalled his father telling him he had placed a robot caterpillar in the memory bank's CPU. Little Busy's remote control could locate the robot caterpillar's position.

Kuan Hee unfolded the remote control in his hand. The screen glowed into life. He recalled his father's instructions as he delved into the hierarchical menu and tapped on different icons. The remote control was indeed complex for the tiny state-of-the-art robot. *Will I be as good as Dad some day?* Kuan Hee wondered. *These nano robots require delicate engineering.*

He brought up the dedicated screen for the robot caterpillar. In a second, the screen switched to a map on which a blinking orange dot stood. *It's somewhere in Sembawang,* he told himself. He pinched the map and spread two fingers to enlarge it. *Let's see now. Sun Plaza...Old Nelson Road,* he muttered under his breath.

He heard faint footsteps in the corridor. Then the door creaked open and Lina came in carrying their breakfast.

"How's the situation outside?"

"People going about doing their own things."

"Any soldiers?"

"Nope. What's that?"

"Getting a fix on the robot caterpillar's position. It's at Old Admiralty House."

"Gosh! That's the PM's residence."

"Yes, seems Colonel Tee only trusts himself. He keeps the memory bank near him."

"It will be heavily guarded. It's dangerous going there." Lina unwrapped the disposable chopsticks and handed a pair to Kuan Hee. They ate fried beehoon together.

"It's on a hill. It is difficult to recce, even more difficult to infiltrate. Anyone up there can see us immediately."

"We've got little Busy."

"But I still have to get up there."

"Oh! I forgot."

"I will do a search on Old Admiralty House. It's a national monument so there should be plenty of information on the place online."

Lina left Kuan Hee alone. She knew he hated to be disturbed when he was on to something. She spent the morning cleaning the room and washing their laundry.

An hour later, she came up behind Kuan Hee. "So how's the progress."

"There's speculation about a secret tunnel somewhere under the house. Seems it leads to Sembawang Shipyard."

"Really? Could be leading us on a wild goose chase."

"I know. But in 1990, during excavation work on the grounds, the contractors discovered an underground bunker—World War II period."

"For real?"

"Yes. It says so in the online national library archives."

The evening brought updates on the police revolt situation on the island. The navy and air force commanders had gone on air to state their neutrality in the on-going conflict. That the news media had given them a chance to air their views on national television spoke volumes about the volatile situation. It was a slap in the face for the Ong Chwee Seng government.

"The police can breathe more easily now."

"Yes. And I can't keep putting off my mission. Time is of the essence. Colonel Tee could move the master tapes anytime. It could go into an army base. That will make finding it more difficult."

"You going to give up looking for the secret tunnel on Old Admiralty House?"

"I have been looking high and low. It's thrown up nothing but dead ends. I don't have the luxury of time. Besides, it might not exist."

"What have you found out so far?"

Kuan Hee and Lina browsed the Websites he had bookmarked in his search. They examined the pictures of the various rooms in the big house and the surroundings.

Lina fingered a large room on the second storey. "So Queen Elizabeth II stayed in this room when she visited Singapore. I bet Colonel Tee must be sleeping in this room too."

"For sure. The memory bank could be in this room. We will send little Busy into the room to look around."

"When are we going to Old Admiralty House?"

"I have completed the research. We can go tomorrow. Remember to bring pen and paper. We are going to sketch a plan of the house."

Early next morning, an Uber car took Kuan Hee and Lina to Sembawang. The driver avoided Sembawang Road where several army camps were sited. Instead, he took them through Yishun Avenue two, which ran smack in the middle of an HDB estate. They passed soldiers guarding MRT stations along the route. There were no roadblocks.

On arrival, the pair staked out Old Admiralty House and watched from a safe distance. They squatted in a drain on the bottom of the hill, outside the perimeter fencing on the far end of the sprawling grounds. It was difficult to see the top of the hill through the trees and the bushes. *Good. People up on the hill can't see us too,* Kuan Hee told himself. He unfolded the remote to reveal the control panel for the robot caterpillar. He tapped on the camera icon. At once, the screen went into video mode. But all the pair could see was a darkened screen.

"Kuan Hee, is the screen working? It's blank."

"Of course, it's working. It's just too dark, I guess. I can't see anything."

"Switch on the caterpillar's lights." Kuan Hee tapped on a flashlight icon. At once, the caterpillar's eyes shone. Its home for the past year lit up.

"Looks like a computer server. We are looking at the innards. Let me try to get out of this contraption." Kuan Hee let the caterpillar wriggle along the metal frame of the computer and then out through a small opening on one side.

"It is inside a metal cabinet of some sort. *Aiyoh*, this caterpillar sure is slow. Little Busy could have done the job in a few seconds."

"Don't complain, Kuan Hee. Your father must have had a good reason for making the caterpillar like that."

"I see marking on the metal wall of the cabinet. Let me zoom in. Says C-H-U-B-B. Gosh! It's a Chubb safe." Kuan Hee stared in disbelief. Then he spoke. "I was going to steal the master tapes. Now, it looks like I have to destroy the whole safe instead. There's no way to get inside the safe."

"So we are looking for a safe? A Chubb safe?"

"Yes. Alex's laser weapon will come in handy."

"But the robot caterpillar's in the safe."

"It's a pity, but I have no choice. It's either the robot caterpillar or the country. I'm sure Dad will understand. Anyway, he's the one who is adamant about destroying the memory bank. He must have known he was putting the robot caterpillar in a death mission."

"You speak as if the caterpillar is alive."

"Finding the master tapes is of paramount importance. Let's release little Busy." Kuan Hee switched to the main menu on little Busy's remote.

Little Busy flitted up the slope. It flew over bushes and trees till it was hovering over a large flat open ground on the top of the hill. A stately old mansion—with wide verandahs on its upper floor, long wooden louvred windows and a gable roof—took centre stage, with two smaller buildings on its right and a swimming pool next to it. Adjacent to them stood a newer building standing on lower ground. Beyond the buildings, on the horizon, a long line of tightly packed blocks of HDB flats met the sky. Two armored personnel carriers dotted the open space near the mansion. There was a smattering of soldiers moving around the grounds.

Lina sketched the layout as the scene played out before them. Kuan Hee manoeuvred little Busy towards the big house. It flew into a large sitting room on the second level. No one was in it. The robot housefly flitted through a long corridor where sunlight glared through tall windows on one side. There were two doors opposite the windows. At the end of the corridor, next to the staircase was another door. According to a Website, this was the room Queen Elizabeth had stayed in when she visited Singapore. Kuan Hee switched to the map screen for the robot caterpillar. The orange dot on the map was flickering in greater intensity.

"The memory bank should be inside this room. But there's no gap for little Busy to sneak through."

"Fly outside the house to the windows of the room."

"Yeah. I forgot about the windows."

"You always do."

Kuan Hee instructed little Busy to fly out the windows up over the roof to the other side of the house. Soon it hovered outside the room's two windows. They were shut.

"The gaps between the lourves are too tiny for little Busy to slip through. Its heat sensors are telling me the air-conditioning is not on. I think nobody's in. At least, we know the tapes are somewhere inside."

"Kuan Hee, move around the place so I can complete my map." Kuan Hee let the robot housefly explore the premises. As it moved around, Lina sketched details onto the map she had drawn.

"The soldiers are concentrated at the entrance on top of the hill. Mark their positions. Also draw circles where the machine guns overlook the bottom of the hill."

In an hour, Lina had finished with the sketched map. They were tired after being in a constricted position for so long.

"We'll come back tomorrow to take care of the memory bank. I miscalculated. I can't tackle the hill alone."

Just then, a motorcade roared into the compound. The Mercedes-Benz moved away from the two Volvos and stopped in the porch. Little Busy reversed direction and flew over the porch. A seventyish man, pompous and rotund, stepped out of the back of the vehicle. He paused to survey the surroundings and then entered the house with two men in army fatigues following him.

"Ong Chwee Seng. That's him all right."

"Are we staying or going?"

"Let's observe him for a while. I will send little Busy after him." Little Busy flew into the house, trailing the men through the corridor on the upper floor. The men went into a room at the other end of the corridor. It perched itself on a painting in the longish room. A large desk and an oversized armchair stood on the side of the door and facing them, across the room, were two tall windows. A settee and armchair occupied the space at the far end of the room.

Ong Chwee Seng sank into the armchair behind his desk. His two lieutenants stood across the desk. Both looked glum. Ong Chwee Seng drew a breath. "Wipe them off the face of the earth."

"But, sir. Who will take charge of the police then?" said the man nearest him. He wore the epaulettes of a Lieutenant General.

"We can put them under the MPs," said Ong Chwee Seng.

"But it's still the military police, sir. People will think they are under military rule," the man protested.

"Aren't they now?" said Ong Chwee Seng. "Look, Warren. We can drop the pretence since some of them no longer support us. Anyway, we don't need them. I will do away with the polls. This police revolt has given me the perfect opportunity."

Warren Tan, a major who followed Colonel Tee into power five years ago was now a Lieutenant General in the army. Somehow, he had escaped the scalping of Colonel Tee's followers, which took place when the Tee Dynasty fell.

The three men huddled over a large map on the desk.

"Pound their positions. Pulverize them," said Ong Chwee Ong, slapping his palm on the map.

"Yes, sir," the two men chorused in unison.

Kuan Hee and Lina had no inkling what the men were discussing. But they were sure it had something to do with the police strongholds. It was too dangerous for little Busy to fly over the men for a closer look.

"Time to withdraw." Kuan Hee got little Busy to fly out of the room back down the hill to where they were squatting. The pair climbed out of the drain clumsily. They had spent an eternity in the drain; their legs were numb.

CHAPTER 31

On the other side of town, along New Bridge Road, a huge procession had taken shape. People from all walks of life had flocked to Chinatown to stand as one against the authoritarian regime of Ong Chwee Seng. They had had enough of his regime. They didn't want to wait four more years for the ballot box to take him down. They wanted him to step down straightaway. The police revolt was timely. It acted as the catalyst for Navin to cobble together a coterie of groups with the common aim of bringing down his regime. From political parties to non-government organisations, almost everyone who's anyone in society was represented.

From Outram Road MRT Station all the way to the Speakers' Corner in Hong Lim Park, it was a sea of faces. It was not easy for Navin to keep the different groups together. Each group's leaders had its own agenda; this uneasy union between the groups at times threatened to throw the protest into disarray. Fortunately, they all hated Ong Chwee Seng enough to keep their differences beneath the surface—for the time being. How did Ong Chwee Seng's popularity spiral downwards in a short span of less than a year? For the answer, look no further than ancient philosopher Aristotle's words:

"No notice is taken of a little evil, but when it
increases it strikes the eye."

"You managed to get these disparate groups together? Impressive. I couldn't have done better myself," said Kuan Hee. Navin beamed.

"It's indeed an achievement, getting First People's Party, One Singapore Party and Unity Party to bury their differences," said Tim.

"*LOL!* The common good makes the difference," said Navin.

"How's the going, Kuan Hee?" asked Tim.

"Not so good *lah*. Need your help. Not now. Tonight," said Kuan Hee. "I can't make it up the hill alone." Kuan Hee described the situation on the hill to the two men. "But I guess Navin's got his hands full here."

"You and I should be enough," said Tim. "But we need hardware. Let me retrieve them first." His eyes did not betray fear.

For their own reasons, the police were anxious to let the protest go smoothly. They were not taking any chances. Their commanders stationed armored multi-purpose vehicles at the junctions along the protest site. Gurkha policemen stood atop their turrets. Their no-nonsense looks reassured the protesters of their safety.

Over at the Gurkha's Mount Vernon Camp—the home of the contingent, the mother of battles had begun. It started with the army's howitzers pounding the grounds. These were self-propelled howitzers mounted on tracked vehicles called Primus. The army had sent two of these vehicles to Vernon Park. Then Bionix armored fighting vehicles rolled up Mount Vernon Road. The Gurkha guards on duty fought a hard fight, trying to keep their attackers at bay. There was no let up in the army's attack. Fortunately, the Gurkha contingent's families were not on site. They had been relocated days before on fears that the army would mount retaliatory action. Nevertheless, there were casualties from the howitzers' pounding. The howitzers did not play fair; they targeted the highrise living quarters of the Gurkhas, blasting holes through the walls.

If the Gurkha policemen along the protest route in New Bridge Road were unsettled by the news of the intense firefight, they certainly did not show it in their faces. They stood steadfast atop their vehicles. For them, allegiance to Singapore came first.

The embattled Gurkhas on Mount Venon did not have to wait long, for the police commanders had sent a convoy of Tenix S600 armored carriers to the rescue. Policemen in them were armed with TOW anti-tank missiles, powerful enough to blow the howitzer-mounted Primuses to smithereens.

The arriving Tenix armored carriers locked the attackers between them and the Gurkhas on Mount Vernon. Policemen leapt out of the vehicles, carrying TOW missile launchers and wielding MP5 sub-machine guns. They fanned out across the slope in front of Mount Vernon Road and stealthily they ascended it. Some fired their TOW anti-tank missiles at the army's Primuses and armored personnel carriers, while others sprayed bullets at the soldiers along Mount Vernon Road. The attackers found themselves stuck between a rock and a hard place.

Taken by surprise, the soldiers yelled in pain, dropping like flies to the ground. Their mission was in peril. Soon the Primuses and armored personnel carriers were but a shell of themselves with plumes of smoke billowing from them. Remnants of the invading force surrendered to the Gurkha policemen.

News of the police's success in fending off the army attack at Mount Vernon Camp spread like wildfire across the protest site. The protesters looked at the Gurkha guards with renewed respect; for the Gurkhas had not flinched from duty.

Standing next to a Gurkha armored carrier stationed outside the historic Yue Hwa Building, the four friends mingled with fellow protesters in the dwindling evening light. The event had gone without a hitch all day. Perhaps, the presence of the fierce-looking Gurkhas had something to do with it. No one knew or cared. Everyone was having a good time, oblivious to the dark clouds looming overhead. *These are night clouds,* the protesters reasoned to themselves.

CHAPTER 32

With nightfall came the city lights, which illuminated the dark skies. Floodlights from portable towers lit up the intersections of roads along the protest site.

It was time for Kuan Hee and Tim to make a move. Leaving Navin and Lina behind, they scrambled into Lina's brother's van parked along Upper Cross Street. Xaden had come along for the ride. He sat in front, next to his father. With its human load tucked in the back, the van cruised along Clemenceau Avenue, heading first to Paya Lebar, where it stopped by Tim's family-owned warehouse. Tim alighted to pick up a large tennis bag. It held two SAR21s and ammunition.

"So this is where you have been hiding the weapons all along."

"It's so big, there's no way anybody will notice a small bag hidden in some nook."

"*Wah!* You are really clever." Tim's face reddened. He took out the SAR21s. These came with 40mm underbarrel grenade launchers locked into place.

"How did you get your hands on these M203s?"

"You like them?"

"Of course *lah*. They are a godsend."

Both men did a quick cleaning of the rifles. Then they slapped the magazines into the magazine well of the rifles and slid the M203 barrel forward. They slotted in a grenade and glided the barrel backwards. Their rifles were now primed for action. They slipped a spare clip and two grenades into their backpacks.

"Two clips—sixty rounds altogether. Should be enough."

"I'll take Alex; Xander will follow you. Here's the headset. It's been programmed to communicate with Xander directly. Kuan Hee retrieved AleXander the robots from his backpack and opened their front panels.

"Follow," Kuan Hee spoke into the headset he had plugged into his ear. "This ensures Alex stays by my side all the time." Tim did the same with his headset.

The van arrived at a desolate road behind the hill.

"We'll be back soon," said Kuan Hee to Lina's brother. Her brother waved them on as he and Xaden surveyed the surroundings.

With their backpacks strapped firmly to their backs, Kuan Hee and Tim climbed the slope together with Alex and Xander, stopping every few steps to watch for the slightest movements on top of the hill. They could not afford to be sloppy, for mistakes could cost them their lives. Kuan Hee released little Busy into the air. The robot housefly flew upwards towards the light. On reaching the top of the hill, little Busy wasted no time in surveying the perimeter of the grounds, looking for machine-gun nests. It found three, one overlooking the open field across the road, another looking down at the overhead MRT tracks and a third only metres on top of them.

Kuan Hee shut the remote and gestured for Tim to move sideways. They inched nearer to where they had started the climb. "We are outmatched."

"It's going to be damned hard to come out of this alive. I'm having second thoughts."

"Don't. Even if we die martyrs, we still have to do the

job."

"*Wahseh*, you haven't even seen your little Huei Huei and you are talking nonsense like this. Cut it out."

"Shush!" Kuan Hee placed a finger over his lips. "Let me think." Minutes slipped by as Kuan Hee contemplated their mission. Then he spoke.

"I'll go up alone. You keep watch here. If I don't return in fifteen minutes, leave this place." Without waiting for a reply, Kuan Hee snuck up the slope with Alex, stealing a quick glance back at Tim before resuming his climb. Then he heard a faint sound behind him. It was Tim. He had changed his mind.

"For better or for worse," Tim whispered. Kuan Hee nodded.

There was no turning back now for the two men. They understood their country came first. They stole past two soldiers manning a machine gun on their right. They crouched down and duckwalked through the verandah of a small building next to the swimming pool.

Seeing no one in the open space between the mansion and them, they sprinted across the open space. They spied a guard at the porch. Kuan Hee gestured for them to take the opposite direction. They crept around the mansion to the back. Kuan Hee tried a door. It opened into a large room empty of people. They sidled to the opening at the other end and peeped into the foyer. The coast was clear. A stately staircase stood on their left. The two men climbed the stairs to the second level. Colonel Tee's bedroom was on their right, next to the staircase. They tried the knob; the door opened and cool air met their faces.

Kuan Hee surveyed the large room while Tim kept an eye on the corridor through a crack in the door. Kuan Hee had precious minutes to complete his task. He could not dillydally. He had to take a risk. "Time for the robot caterpillar to make a noise." He tapped on the loudhailer icon on the remote. At once a piercing beep resonated in the room. It seemed to come from the king-sized bed. He walked to the bed and knelt beside it. There was nothing suspicious about the divan or the mattress. The large wooden headboard had to conceal something. He leaned the rifle against the wall and pushed the bed away from him.

Embedded in the wall was a rectangular old-world safe. It had an oval brass plate with the words C-H-U-B-B emblazoned on it. Directly below the inscription, there was a combination lock and a handle. *This is it,* Kuan Hee told himself. *The memory bank must be in it.*

There was no way Kuan Hee could open the safe. Even if he could pry it off the wall, it looked too heavy to lug away. *Have to say goodbye to the robot caterpillar,* he told himself. *Sorry, old chap. I have no choice.*

He thought about using the M203 on his rifle, but decided against it. It might not be able to blast the safe to bits. He did not have time for a second try. He had to make the first work. He grabbed his rifle and stood away from the safe. Then he retreated to the far end of the room, next to Tim. *Play safe,* he told himself. He tapped Tim's shoulder. Tim nodded. They braced themselves for the explosion that would follow.

"Destroy-fire-1," he commanded Alex. He had used Alex's most potent weapon. It had the power to tear a gaping hole through a tank. Alex remained standing with his feet apart. It had readied itself for action, but nothing happened.

"Kuan Hee," Tim whispered. "What's wrong?"

"*Alamak!*" Kuan Hee blurted out. "Did I forget something?" He had been nervous and didn't realize he had forgotten to open Alex's front panel. It was a safety feature that his father had incorporated into the two robots.

"*Ah!*" Kuan Hee exclaimed. He knelt next to Alex and opened its front panel. "Alex, destroy-fire-1."

At once, Alex's laser weapon system went into gear. It

unleashed a blinding beam that illuminated the whole room. Its high-energy laser hit the Chubb safe, combusting it in seconds, and ripping a large hole in the wall. All that was left of the safe was a melted heap of white-hot metal.

There was the sound of footsteps running outside the room and in the compound outside. Their rifles at the ready, Kuan Hee and Tim dashed out of the door, with the two robots at their heels.

They returned fire at the soldiers running through the corridor. They clambered down the stairs, firing at the soldiers below. Tim lobbed a grenade with his M203. The soldiers at the porch fell.

The whole hill had awakened. Soldiers were running across the compound. They came out of nowhere. *There has to be a garrison stationed here,* Tim told himself. The two men ran like they never ran before, back to the small building next to the swimming pool, and then the grassy verge.

Behind them, bullets rained. Then the two men crouched below a low parapet wall. Machine gun fire was spraying the walls with holes. They had forgotten about the nest ahead of them. While Tim was firing at the soldiers behind them, Kuan Hee released the M203's safety catch and lobbed a grenade into the machine gun nest. At once there was silence in the darkness ahead.

The two men scurried into the darkness, and clambered down the slope, leaving their pursuers bewildered.

Suddenly, Kuan Hee fell and rolled down the slope. He had been shot. By then, Tim had almost reached the bottom of the slope; he was a better runner. He heard a loud thud sound behind and turned to take a look. Kuan Hee was not to be seen but there was a limp figure on the grass up ahead. He retraced his steps towards where the figure lay. But it was too late, for soldiers were hovering around the figure. In the darkness, he could not take them alone, not without harming Kuan Hee.

Tim retreated down the hill and ran towards the parked

van. With him safely inside, the van sped off.

When Kuan Hee came to, he found himself seated in a chair in a small room. He felt faint. His hands were tied behind him. He felt cold metal pressing on his wrists. Blood seeped through a hastily bundled bandage wrapped across his back. Standing in front of him was a soldier in fatigues, wearing the epaulettes of a Colonel. He had a thick round face, unshaven at the chin.

"Ah, I see you are conscious now," the Colonel said in a gruff voice. He pulled a chair in front of him and sat in it. His eyes met Kuan Hee's. "Very brave chap, you. Young too. Who sent you?" There was silence in the room. Then the Colonel broke the silence by slapping Kuan Hee's face with a heavy calloused palm. He repeated the slaps. Kuan Hee's lips bled, but he remained defiantly quiet. The pain was also gnawing at the flesh in his back. *I have to remain strong,* he told himself.

The door opened and Ong Chwee Seng stepped into the room. Behind him was Lieutenant General Warren Tan.

"Did you get anything out of him?" Ong Chwee Seng asked.

"No, sir. Not yet. This young chap is stubborn, very stubborn, sir," said the Colonel.

"Is he badly hurt?" Ong Chwee Seng asked.

"Bullet lodged in his back. I've stopped the bleeding for the time being, sir," said the Colonel. "He's got gunshot scars on his body. Looks like he's battle-hardened, sir."

"What? Really? He's such a young lad," said Ong Chwee Seng. "Amazing." He stooped to take a closer look at his prisoner. "You look familiar. I've seen you before, somewhere." He grabbed Kuan Hee's hair and tilted the young intruder's head.

"*Ah.* I remember now. I have seen your picture somewhere. Yes, you are Professor Wang's son—his only son." He let go of Kuan Hee's hair and stood in front of him, hands clasping both sides of his waist.

"No doubt about it. You are Professor Wang's son, all right. Your father escaped from me and went into hiding. I thought all was lost." Ong Chwee Seng let out a haunting laugh. "Your father will come running back to me once I let word out you are in my custody."

"Sir, he must have come for the master tapes," said Lietenant General Warren Tan. Ong Chwee Seng's face contorted with fury. He grabbed Kuan Hee's sides and lifted him off the chair. Kuan Hee grimaced in pain. His back was hurting badly.

"You destroyed my memories, you little devil," Ong Chwee Seng screamed.

Suddenly, he recalled seeing Kuan Hee at Singapore General Hospital where his son had been warded five years ago. Pain tore through his heart when he realized Kuan Hee was the one who was responsible for his son's death.

"You—you are the one who killed my son—my precious son."

"No! You killed Jordan," said Kuan Hee in a weak voice. At once, he poured out his grievances. "You killed your own son! It was your greed. For the sake of power, you lived in his mind. You tormented his mind with your evil deeds. He wanted you to repent but you became worse. The only way to deal with you was for him to kill himself. He saved Singapore."

"No! No! You are lying. You are lying through your teeth. I will teach you a lesson today or my name is not Tee Bak Chai."

"Of course you aren't Tee Bak Chai. You are Ong Chwee Seng."

"Smart aleck!" Ong Chwee Seng screamed. He reached for the Colonel's holster. He pulled the pistol out and pointed it at Kuan Hee's head.

"Jordan. My son, can you hear me?" Ong Chwee Seng wailed. "I will avenge you today, Jordan." His finger squeezed the trigger.

Kuan Hee's face turned white with fear. In a second, he would be dead. He braced himself for the bullet he would take in his head. Then he spied Alex lying on the floor in a corner, with its front panel resting at an angle against the floor. He screamed his lungs out. "Alex, arouse-hit-fire-3."

At once, Alex woke up. It rolled onto the floor, kicked itself into an upright stance, and sprang into action, firing its lasers at the three men in the room. They fell into a heap on the floor, their bodies smouldering through their tattered clothes.

It was all over. Ong Chwee Seng and his minions had been killed. Singapore was free again.

Kuan Hee fell off the chair. He got up and staggered to the door. With his hands still handcuffed behind him, he tried to open the door. He was too weak to turn the knob. "Alex, hit-fire-1." Alex's laser blasted the door open. Kuan Hee poked his head outside. He was in the verandah, on the ground floor of a small building. He wobbled along the corridor towards the grassy slope with Alex at his heels. Soldiers were running towards him. He had hardly any strength left to run; he was a sitting duck. *My mission has been accomplished,* Kuan Hee told himself. He was resigned to his fate. *I am at peace.* He fell to the ground.

CHAPTER 33

Kuan Hee heard voices around him. Some sounded familiar. *Am I dead? Am I in heaven or in hell?* His thoughts tormented him. His eyeballs moved erratically. *Lina. My Lina. Huei Huei. Where are you?* He cried out in his thoughts. He saw them in front of him and tried to reach out to them. They were so near, yet so far away. He tried to grab their hands but no matter how hard he tried, he could not move an inch. Something was holding him back. He was moving farther away from his beloved Lina and Huei Huei. *It's the shackles. It is pulling me back everytime I try to move forward.* He tried with all his might. At last, he broke free of the shackles. At once, darkness turned into daylight. *How wonderful,* he told himself. But it was too bright. His eyes were uncomfortable in the bright light.

Kuan Hee squinted his eyes. Then he opened them. He saw Lina by his side. She was cuddling a baby—his beloved Huei Huei. He glanced around the room. He saw Tim and Navin. "Where am I?"

"Kuan Hee, you are awake. Thank heavens you are awake at last," said Lina. She leaned against him and planted a kiss on his forehead.

"I knew you would pull through," said Tim. He was

fighting back tears. "I'm so sorry I left you behind."

"Kuan Hee, so good to see you again," said Navin. He slapped Kuan Hee's shoulder playfully.

"What happened?" said Kuan Hee. He realized he was in a hospital ward. Navin cranked up the head of the bed so Kuan Hee could sit up. He looked out of the tall window on his left. The sun was gawking at him. *It must be indignant that I have slept so long, while it has to work hard to keep the world bright,* he told himself.

"How long have I been out?" Kuan Hee asked. His three questions had gotten no answers so far. He tried again.

"I thought I was dead," Kuan Hee said. "How did I get here? Won't someone tell me?"

At this moment, the door opened and Brigadier Walmsley stepped into the room. He stood next to Lina.

"By George, you are all right," said the Brigadier. "Sure got all of us worried sick. Don't do it again, young lad."

"Mr Walmsley, you are here," said Kuan Hee.

"You are looking good, old chap," said the Brigadier. "Let me see now. If I am not wrong, it's the fourth time you have been shot. You should be getting a medal for every one of your bullet scars."

"Mr Walmsley, you are horrid, simply horrid," said Lina. She was close to tears.

"Lina, he's only jesting," said Tim. "Anyone can see he's joking."

"My dear girl, you are indeed too sensitive," said the Brigadier. "Kuan Hee's in for hard times, for sure."

"Mr Walmsley, do you know what happened to me?" asked Kuan Hee. "I've been trying to get them to tell me, but no one has said anything."

"Kuan Hee. It's a long story," said the Brigadier. "In a nutshell, the delta force got you out of a jam."

"Delta force?" said Kuan Hee. "You mean they were around when I fell?"

"Of course, old chap," said the Brigadier. "To tell you

the truth, I didn't really trust you to get the job done. So I got them to tail you—report your every move. The commandoes were nearby when you and your friend here tried to be heroes on your own."

"You mean, they were on the hill too?" said Kuan Hee.

"Well, not at first. They came a little later," said the Brigadier. "I'm sorry we took so long. You know, taking action in a foreign land is a complicated thing. Need to get permissions from the top and all that. But it didn't really take that long. Our Apache helicopters took care of things on the hill that night. Our commandoes cleaned up the mess after you fell. The important thing is. All's well right now."

"Yes, Mr Walmsley is right," said Tim. "What counts is we are all together safe and sound."

"How about Singapore?" asked Kuan Hee. "Who's in charge now?"

"We are," said Tim. "The people of Singapore are finally in charge."

The End

Some of the places mentioned in this book are real:

Battle Box
Capitol Building
CHIJMES
Dieppe Barracks
Fort Canning Hill
Jalan Naung
Hougang Avenue five
Istana
Khatib Camp
King George's Avenue
Lavender Street
MacDonald's House
Marina Square Shopping Mall
Mount Vernon Camp
MRT Stations
Nee Soon Camp
New Phoenix Park
Old Admiralty House
Realty Park
SAFTI — Singapore Armed Forces Training Institute
The Float@Marina
Tyrwhitt Road building — old Victoria School
YMCA Building, Orchard Road
Yue Hwa Building

Temasek University in Yio Chu Kang is a figment of the author's imagination. So is the Colonial Hotel.

SINGLISH AND OTHER TERMS USED

ah: added to the end of a sentence for emphasis
Ah Ma: Hokkien for grandmother
aiyah: expressing shock or astonishment
aiyoh: expressing shock or astonishment
alamak: expressing regret, shock or astonishment
chapati: wholemeal pancake cooked on the griddle
choy: Cantonese interjection, similar to 'touch wood'
gostan: moving in reverse direction
GTG: got to go
hentak-kaki: Malay for marching on the spot
Hokkien: a Chinese dialect
hor: added to the end of a sentence for emphasis
IDK: I don't know
kakis: Malay for buddies
Kangkong Belacan: water spinach with shrimp paste
kapoh: being a busybody
kiasi: aversive to risk taking
kiasu: afraid of losing out to others
kopi oh kosong: Malay for black coffee, no sugar added
lah: added to the end of a sentence for emphasis
leh: added to the end of a sentence for emphasis
LOL: acronym for 'Laughing Out Loud'
NSmen: National Service men
ORD: operationally ready date (completed NS)
ponteng: skip/play truant
roti prata: pan-fried flat bread
sambal belacan: a shrimp paste used in Malay cuisine
three-tonner: a military truck (weighs three tonnes)
wah: expressing shock or surprise
wah piang: expressing shock
wah seh: expressing shock

The author lives with his wife in an HDB flat in Hougang, an idyllic backwater in the North-East of Singapore. They have no children.

ABOUT THE AUTHOR

Raymond Han is a late baby boomer in Singapore. He has worked as a banker, an editor, and a teacher. After he left the banking sector, he found a second career teaching English Language to upper and lower secondary students in Victoria School, Montfort Secondary School, Greendale Secondary School and Hougang Secondary School.

Raymond also taught English at 'O' Level and General Paper to students in a private school for several years. He has a Specialist Diploma in Psychology (Counselling Psychology).

Besides teaching, Raymond has written four books for young adults. The first, a short-story compilation entitled 'Spice of Life: Singapore Short Stories', traces the trials and tribulations of some ordinary youngsters living in different periods of time in Singapore's modern history, from the late sixties and early seventies, through to the eighties and nineties. The second, 'Essential Guide to O-level English Composition', aims to help students build a systematic approach to tackling essay writing for the GCE O-level English Language paper. It incorporates a step-by-step method to teach students to write better paragraphs and essays. The third, 'Mystery of the Battlebox', his maiden novel, is about some teenagers falling into adventure and discovering hidden gold. And the fourth, 'Where the Wind Blows', describes the adventures of a group of twenty-somethings who pit their intelligence and skills to save Singapore from the clutches of a dictator.